"You're The Princess Who Lives In The Castle."

"And are you the king, or merely a prince?"

He grinned and shook his head. "That would make me either your father or your brother, and I don't want to waste my imagination being either."

She moistened her lips and held her breath before she asked, "What *would* you like to be?"

His expression sobered, and his gaze rested on her mouth. "I think you already know the answer to that question."

Rob's whispering voice sent Sharon's mind spinning, not to mention what it did to her blood pressure. She felt herself being drawn closer to him, helpless to stem the flow of physical need she neither wanted nor understood. For endless minutes his eyes were locked with hers, and then his long lashes hid the darkening of his searching glance.

Dear Reader,

Welcome to Silhouette! Our goal is to give you hours of unbeatable reading pleasure, and we hope you'll enjoy each month's six new Silhouette Desires. These sensual, provocative love stories are both believable and compelling—sometimes they're poignant, sometimes humorous, but always enjoyable.

Indulge yourself. Experience all the passion and excitement of falling in love along with our heroine as she meets the irresistible man of her dreams and together they overcome all obstacles in the path to a happy ending.

If this is your first Desire, I hope it'll be the first of many. If you're already a Silhouette Desire reader, thanks for your support! Look for some of your favorite authors in the coming months: Stephanie James, Diana Palmer, Dixie Browning, Ann Major and Doreen Owens Malek, to name just a few.

Happy reading!

Isabel Swift
Senior Editor

NICOLE MONET
The Sandcastle Man

Silhouette Desire

Published by Silhouette Books New York

America's Publisher of Contemporary Romance

SILHOUETTE BOOKS
300 E. 42nd St., New York, N.Y. 10017

Copyright © 1986 by Noelle Berry McCue

ISBN: 0-373-05266-9

First Silhouette Books printing March 1986

America's Publisher of Contemporary Romance

Printed in the U.S.A.

Books by Nicole Monet

Silhouette Desire

NICOLE MONET,

an inveterate writer of romance, lives in California with her husband and daughter and makes of her writing a full-time career. "I write," the author says, "because I am a voracious reader, and I feel that in some small way, I'm paying back all the pleasure I've received in my lifetime."

One

SharonVecchio paced back and forth across her living room carpet, her hands clasped at her waist. She noticed the trembling of her fingers without surprise. Why wouldn't they shake? she thought. She had just returned from a consultation appointment with a sperm bank, for heaven's sake! When she considered the enormity of the step she'd just taken, her emotions fluctuated with a combination of incredulity and mild hysteria.

"I want to have a baby," she whispered aloud, as though the words were a magic chant that would give her her heart's desire. Taken by itself, the sentiment she'd expressed wasn't unusual. Many women discovered belated maternal instincts as they approached their thirties and decided to opt for motherhood while they were still physically able.

But for Sharon the instincts weren't belated, merely repressed. She'd carved out a career, first as an army cook, and later as part owner of a restaurant shared with her younger sister, Marilyn, and their friend Casey. Those were busy and self-satisfying years, yet she had always been conscious of something missing from her life. She'd occasionally dated several very nice men, but a vital ingredient had been absent from those relationships. None of them had made her heart beat faster, or caused the heat of desire to run through her veins. Eventually the relationships drifted into comfortable friendships, and she'd continued her life without a moment's regret.

Drawing a calming breath into her lungs, Sharon stopped to inspect her surroundings. She studied the beautiful English chintz covering her sofa, the background a rich tan that matched the carpeting. The overall pattern consisted of pale rose and gold flowers linked with delicate greenery. The design had a joyful, summery air, which was enhanced by a hand-woven basket of straw flowers and a cluster of porcelain figurines on an adjoining oak drum table.

The living room had the warm ambience of a well-maintained home, and yet for Sharon it only accentuated her loneliness. Home is where the heart is, she thought, her eyes mirroring the emptiness that had begun to eat at her soul. For her a home meant the companionship of loved ones, not a solitary existence

bereft of any real joy. Her mouth hardened with res-
olution. A home meant children!

With a muttered exclamation she turned and headed
for her kitchenette. Grabbing her favorite mug, she felt
slightly more cheerful as she poured herself some coffee. The front of the cup bore the words "You're out-
standing in your field," and the back showed a cow
standing in an empty field with a disgusted expression
on its face. To finance her own restaurant in Mill Valley, she'd sold her share in their Pleasanton restaurant to her sister and Casey. On the day of the grand
opening of Another Touch of Italy, the two gleeful
idiots had arrived bearing the mug and a bottle of
champagne.

Still smiling at the memory, Sharon slid open the
sliding glass doors that separated her dining area from
the small, postage-sized patio that served as her backyard. The overhanging balcony from the shake roof
provided shade, and the rather ordinary wooden ban-
ister ensured her privacy. She looked down at the
beach from her upstairs apartment. Normally she took
pleasure in watching the people pass by, but today she
felt unsettled. Her depression returned as she gazed at
the shoreline through narrowed eyes.

There were only a handful of units in her apartment building, and all were surrounded by a wooden
fence with a wrought iron gate in both the back, which
opened onto the beach, and the front, which over-
looked the parking area. She let her gaze shift toward
the gate, and her view of the dark, twisted metal suited

her introspective mood. It was a symbol of the emotional prison door she'd locked herself behind for so many lonely years, she thought.

Sharon winced at the comparison, and her hands tightened around the mug she held. She hadn't always lived such a solitary existence. She'd grown up in a loving environment, the oldest of four children. She'd been a shy little girl who was happiest helping her mother around the house. Those days spent as a carefree child had been good and had strengthened her for what was to come.

She'd grown up too quickly, she thought, and yet she hadn't been given a choice. Childish dreams had been discarded shortly after her twelfth birthday when her mother had died. Sharon sighed, wondering if her life would have taken on a better balance if she hadn't had to deal with her grief by taking on a responsibility too heavy for her young shoulders.

For the next six years she'd been both a surrogate mother and a sister to Marilyn and her brothers Paul and Eric. But then her father was injured in an automobile accident, and when she realized he would be on permanent disability, she'd been forced into making the most difficult decision of her life. Right after her graduation from high school she had joined the army. Her desire to help her father with the expense of educating her younger siblings overcame her reluctance to leave home.

In the beginning she thought she would die of homesickness, but she survived boot camp. When she was permanently stationed at Fort Ord, close enough to home for her to visit her family when she had leave, she finally adjusted to military life. She hadn't known then that she was shortly to experience a happiness greater than anything she had ever known. *Michael....*

Her mind whispered his name as her thoughts swept backward in time until the image of curly red hair and laughing blue eyes became clear. They had dreamed of a future together, and the time they'd managed to share alone had been precious. His arms had become her haven, and she had clung to the promises they'd made to each other when he was sent to Vietnam. Those dreams had died with him.

The sound of voices broke into her reveries, and it was only then that Sharon became aware of the tears trickling down her cheeks. A young woman passed by, dragging a protesting, sand-encrusted little boy. Sharon quickly set the mug down on her patio table and wiped away her tears with self-conscious thoroughness. The sight of the child was a vivid reminder of her visit to the sperm bank, and she was suddenly unable to cope with the worrisome thoughts racing around in her head.

Quickly she turned and reentered her apartment. Feeling driven, she passed through her living room and found herself on the upper landing overlooking the pool. She rushed down the cement steps and reached out to release the catch on the gate. Turning the corner she climbed down a narrow path and stepped out onto the sandy beach. When the ocean breeze tugged at her clothing, she threw her head back to savor the salt-laden air.

Her black shoulder-length hair was restrained in a French twist at the back of her neck, but several strands escaped to be whipped into wild disarray. She brushed them from her mouth, and her dark eyes reflected the relief she felt at the distraction. She could cope with the elements. Nature was one of life's constants, she thought, the weather changing to enhance each new season. She only wished she were as agreeable to the changes taking place in her own life.

As she walked she tried to come to terms with the decision she'd made for her future. Was she really capable of guiding not only her own destiny but that of a child? And what of later, she thought, nibbling at her lower lip. How would she respond when asked about the man who'd fathered her child? What would she tell her son or daughter!

The questions were endless and as Sharon walked slowly along the shore she couldn't find easy answers. Yet in trying to anticipate future difficulties, wasn't she being unnecessarily hard on herself? At twenty-nine she was still young and healthy enough to safely carry a baby to term. Also, material necessities would not pose a problem. Her restaurant was doing well, even though it had been open for only six months. Okay, she thought, with a return of her usual self-confidence, those were definitely two points in her favor.

Summing up her thoughts, Sharon came to the conclusions that she was healthy, a successful businesswoman and no stranger to responsibility. Last, but by no means least, she had an untapped fountain of love inside of her just aching to be shared with a child.

Her bare feet moved faster over the coolness of the surf-dampened sand. In a bulky gray sweatshirt and ragged cutoff jeans she looked as if she fitted in with the few people left frolicking by the shore. But Sharon felt set apart by the knowledge of her own loneliness and was impatient with her tumultuous thoughts. She walked on, never noticing the beach becoming deserted as evening began to descend.

A gust of wind gathered its chill from the ocean, and she shivered. She'd come much farther than she'd intended and was exhausted by both the walk and her unsolved problems. Feeling cold, she wrapped her arms around her upper body and turned to retrace her footsteps. The peace and contentment she usually found when communing with nature was missing, and she felt somehow cheated. Mentally she chided herself for expecting instant answers to questions that deserved more than brief consideration. Quit torturing yourself, she thought rebelliously. You've been placed on a long waiting list. You'll have plenty of time to make up your mind before the clinic contacts you.

The wind was buffeting the shore in earnest now, and the holiday crowd that had provided a certain amount of company during her walk had sought shelter from the elements. They had the sense to know when to leave, she thought, disgusted by her own lack of foresight. She'd lived here for more than six months and was well aware of the unpredictability of the weather. While she'd been preoccupied with her thoughts a cold, damp fog had descended without warning. When the fog coupled with the mists spewed by the incoming tide, she knew she would be drenched by the time she got home.

Sorry that she hadn't remembered to bring the heavy windbreaker left hanging in her hall closet, Sharon moved farther away from the sea. Although walking on dry sand would leave her legs aching from exertion, she knew she would find some relief from the wind. With determined strides she circled a large rock and stumbled to a halt. Her attention was drawn to a man a few feet away. He was so intent on shaping an exquisite castle from the sand that he was unaware of her presence.

With growing enchantment Sharon studied the capable hands that molded the fairy-tale structure. They were large and browned from exposure to the sun. Yet there was sensitivity in those long fingers, she thought, as they brought his imagined Camelot to life before her eyes. Sharon felt no nervousness at being alone on the beach with a stranger. Something about the man seemed to reach out to her, and any fears she might have felt were as nebulous as the gray wisps swirling in the sky above. Her troubled mind responded to the aura of timelessness that seemed to envelope both her and the sandcastle man, and she felt an inexplicable urge to brush the gold, tumbled hair from his broad brow.

Her heartbeat quickened, and she caught her breath as her skin flushed with sudden heat. Her eyes moved to his wrists and up the muscle-corded arms revealed by his sleeveless sweatshirt. He wore cutoff jeans even more ragged than her own, and as he shifted his weight she saw the tendons bulge in his thighs. Sharon gasped out loud and the man responded to the sound, lifting and pinioning her with eyes as green as a sunlight-dappled sea.

For endless minutes Sharon felt herself trapped by his gaze, an element of awareness leaping between them she was loath to acknowledge. His body slowly straightened, the wide fan of his shoulders etching their imprint against the gathering darkness. He was a large man, and yet he moved with such natural grace that Sharon found herself wondering about the masculine beauty hidden by his clothing. Another gasp emerged through her parted lips, this time one of embarrassment. The dreamlike haze that had taken hold of her consciousness lifted, and she was appalled at the direction her mind was taking.

Afraid her thoughts might be reflected on her face, she turned to leave. But her body had been still for too long and her movements were clumsy as she rushed to escape. With a pained cry she plummeted to the ground, her hands cradling the foot she'd bruised against a protruding rock. A tall shadow momentarily covered her body, and then the sandcastle man was squatting beside her, his cool hands searching her ankle.

When she flinched from his touch, a voice deepened with concern soothed her. "I'm just checking to see if you've broken anything."

"I ... I'm all right," she said, her teeth chattering with a combination of shock and the delight caused by the touch of his fingers. "Anyway, it was my foot I hurt, not my ankle."

He lifted her foot and rested her heel against his naked thigh. Sharon began to tremble at the contact, and she gazed down at his hands examining her foot. Suddenly he stopped. Before she could avert her eyes his head lifted, a gradual smile sweetening the bold curve of his mouth. "It's just a bruise," he said, his expression gentle as he searched her face. "The pain should ease in a minute."

"Thank you, but I feel more embarrassment than pain."

"Why should you be embarrassed?"

Her lashes flickered with shy hesitation. "Because I ... I intruded on your solitude," she stammered, her nervousness increasing as she stood and discovered her head barely reached the middle of his chest. "I'm sorry for troubling you."

This time keeping her eyes on the ground, Sharon began to walk away, but was stopped by his voice. "You didn't, you know."

Turning, she gazed at him, encountering again the sorcery of his smile. "I beg your pardon?"

His grin widened as though he knew her own lips would be unable to resist a response. His glance was drawn to their upward curve, his words a mere whisper as he said, "You didn't intrude upon my solitude."

At a loss for words, Sharon nodded an acknowledgment before finally managing to mutter, "I'm glad."

Silence fell between them, and she felt her embarrassment deepen. Here she was, she thought in disgust, staring calf-eyed at a perfect stranger while her tongue tied itself into one gigantic knot. She wished she could disappear. She wished the encroaching tide would wash her away. She wished—she wished he'd never stop smiling at her.

"My name's Rob."

"Mine's Sharon," she replied softly.

Much to her relief, the exchange of their names eased the tension between them. As though she had known Rob all of her life, she pointed to the sandcastle and smiled. "Are you recapturing your childhood?"

He chuckled and returned to a kneeling position beside his creation. "In a way," he answered truthfully. "For me, building sandcastles is therapeutic. When day-to-day pressures get me down I escape to the beach."

Sharon nodded. "You're lucky to have found a way to handle stress. A lot of the people I know take medication to calm their nerves and then end up more depressed than before. I've never been able to understand that."

"What's your solution, Sharon?"

"Can't you guess?"

Rob responded to the teasing inflection in her voice with a crooked grin, then lowered his eyes to her bare feet. "You come to the beach to run off your troubles?"

"You're close," she said, glancing down at her thighs with a rueful grimace. "I *walk* along the beach. If I ran, I wouldn't have so much extra cushioning around my bones."

"On you the extra cushioning looks good."

Lifting her head in time to see his emerald eyes roam over her body with masculine thoroughness, Sharon became paralyzed with shyness. With self-conscious jerkiness she knelt beside him, deciding an argument would at least keep her tongue in working order. "On me the extra cushioning looks fat."

A single curled finger lifted her chin until their faces were level. "Don't put yourself down, Sharon. You're pleasingly plump... very pleasingly. Not all men appreciate flat chests and bony hips."

Sharon's color rose, her dusky complexion enhanced by apple bright cheeks. Desperate for a change of subject, she murmured, "Can I help you finish your sandcastle?"

His green eyes sparkled with amused comprehension as he moved away, placing a bucket of wet sand within easy reach of their hands. "We'll have to hurry and finish the moat. It'll be dark soon."

Sharon watched Rob begin to shape the outside walls of the castle before she carefully imitated his movements. As they worked a comfortable silence settled between them, and she forgot about being cold. Instead a delicious inner warmth added to her contentment. When the last grains of sand were patted into place, the setting sun had filtered through the descending fog bank, splashing the horizon with an amber glow. Getting slowly to her feet, Sharon stretched her cramped muscles and stared down at the ground. "How long before this part of the beach is under water, Rob?"

"Sometime around midnight, I think."

"I wish we could hold back the tide."

Rising to stand beside her, he placed a consoling arm around her shoulders. "When I was a boy I was a dreamer, and I often wished for the impossible," he admitted with a smile. "My grandmother used to tell me, 'If wishes were horses, beggars would ride.' It irritated the hell out of me."

"I can understand why," she retorted with a giggle. "Children become frustrated when their logic is questioned. A friend of mine has a six-year-old son, and the extent of his imagination is fascinating. We took him to see *Superman III* a couple of years ago, and he came out of the theater thoroughly convinced he was really an alien child from another planet. Casey was afraid he'd jump off the roof to prove he could fly. She nearly had a nervous breakdown before he changed his mind and decided he really wanted to be a geologist. She told me she would rather spend the rest of her life vacuuming rocks than go through that again."

"He sounds like quite a kid."

Sharon's mouth curved in a tender slant. "He is," she said softly. "Jon wouldn't think my wish was silly. He would understand why I can't stand the thought of the sea washing everything away."

"You're not silly, Sharon."

He turned her until she faced him, his strong hands gripping her shoulders. "Nor are you a beggar," he added with winsome appeal. "You're the princess who lives in the castle."

"And are you the king, or merely a prince?"

He grinned and shook his head. "That would make me either your father or your brother, and I don't want to waste my imagination being either."

She moistened her lips with the tip of her tongue, and held her breath before she asked, "What would you like to be?"

"I think you already know the answer to that question."

Rob's whispering voice sent her mind spinning, not to mention what it did to her blood pressure. What in the world had come over her to make her ask such a thing? she thought. She felt herself being drawn closer to him, helpless to stem the flow of physical need she neither wanted nor understood. His arms slipped around to the small of her back, and she shivered as the heat of his body surrounded her.

She wanted to escape his embrace, but her hands misinterpreted the signals from her brain, fascinated with the size and shape of him. Instead of pushing him away, she uncurled her fingers and smoothed her palms against his chest. For endless minutes their eyes locked, then his long lashes hid the darkening of his searching glance.

The mouth that gently rested against hers was cold from the weather, and yet its touch burned through her. Rob didn't try to deepen the kiss; he understood the sudden rigidity of her body without her needing to put her reluctance into words. Instead his lips brushed against hers with a sensitivity that struck at her soul. When his tongue began to tickle the corner of her mouth, she shifted her hands to brace herself against him, her fingers trembling with unexpected delight.

"Sharon..."

"I—I think I'd better be going now."

"Let me walk you back."

Although there was a hint of demand in his offer, he didn't refuse to release her when she discovered a hidden reservoir of determination and pulled herself out of his arms. Her reaction to his kiss had come as a shock, and as she looked at him, she asked herself why he had the power to disturb her to such an extent. She didn't like being out of control and knew she must make him aware of how she felt without further delay. "I'm sorry if I've given you the wrong impression," she said stiltedly. "I—that kiss was a mistake."

"It didn't feel that way to me, Sharon."

When she heard the challenge in his rejoinder she mentally distanced herself. She took a step backward and gazed at him calmly. Only she was aware of the confusion of her mind, she thought, gaining strength from the knowledge. It wouldn't do for this man to discover the nervousness causing her stomach to churn. With a great deal of inward struggle she straightened her spine in an outward show of command. "I'm not looking for an involvement, Rob."

He glanced across the distance separating them. "Is there someone else in your life?"

She resented the question yet felt he deserved an answer. "There was someone a long time ago," she admitted quietly. "Michael died in Vietnam."

"I'm sorry."

The sound of Michael's name on her lips reinforced her need to retreat from the attraction she felt for this man. He was intruding on her space, invading an area of her life she held sacrosanct. With an impersonal nod she said, "Goodbye, Rob. I enjoyed helping you with your sandcastle."

His smile was politely controlled, and yet his eyes held an appeal she couldn't walk away from. "Can I talk you into coming back tomorrow?" he asked.

"I don't think I—"

He reached for her hand, and she forgot what she was going to say. "Couldn't we be friends, Sharon?"

She moistened her dry lips and whispered, "I don't know."

"You could help me build another sandcastle," he said, giving her hand a gentle squeeze before releasing it. "What do you say?"

She hesitated before answering and gnawed nervously at her bottom lip. "I . . . I'll think about it."

His eyes clouded at the evasiveness of her reply, and the smile he gave her held a hint of desperation. "Won't you let me see you home, Sharon?"

Sharon suddenly understood her reluctance to let Rob know where she lived. To her he seemed larger than life, a fantasy figure who had no place in reality. He was offering friendship, and though she desperately needed to find an outlet for her loneliness, she was wary. With Rob she could briefly escape from responsibility and break free from the restrictive pattern of her life. But wouldn't the attraction she felt toward him put her emotional welfare in jeopardy? She didn't know if she could be satisfied with a simple friendship, and the thought frightened her into saying, "I'll be all right, Rob. I don't live far from here."

Her home was nearly a mile away, and Sharon couldn't begin to justify the lie. All she knew was that this stranger had reached inside of her to a place she had thought inviolate. Only Michael had ever touched the tender core of her womanhood, and she felt a sudden surge of resentment. That Rob, a man she hadn't known existed an hour ago, could break through her defenses so easily made her want to run and hide.

"You shouldn't be wandering around alone after dark."

"I can take care of myself."

Rob raked his hand through his hair and emitted a groan of exasperation. "I'm not questioning your independence, woman!"

"Don't spoil it," she whispered, closing her eyes and swallowing hard against the emotion blocking her throat.

He shrugged, his gaze rueful. "Am I coming on too strong again?"

Sharon didn't bother to answer the question. How could she make him understand her reluctance to have him come too close? By withholding her last name and any other details of her life, she was buying the time she desperately needed to sort through her confusion. It was then she faced her fear, not of him, but of herself. The thought of involvement made her feel panic-stricken. She had loved once, and Michael's death had left her life desolate. She was terrified of the pain she knew loving could bring.

Rob was reaching past the fantasy they'd shared to the reality waiting just beyond and it wasn't what she wanted! Then what is it you expect from him? she thought, her conscience prodding her unmercifully. Unable to answer her unspoken question, she took the easy way out. With a muffled goodbye she stepped into the enveloping darkness. She heard him call her name, but she didn't halt her stumbling progress. Once again he called to her, his voice distorted by the damp fog that hid her from his eyes. The sound rippled on the buffeting wind as she hurried across the sand. She was suddenly desperate to reach home. Among familiar surroundings she might be able to forget they'd ever met.

Two

Sharon's rest that night was disturbed by dreams of a smiling man with beckoning eyes and sun-kissed hair. She tossed and turned through the hours until dawn and awakened more tired than when she'd gone to sleep. When she dragged herself out of bed she knew she had to keep busy or go completely around the bend. With determination she stripped off her nightgown and dumped it into the clothes hamper which stood just inside the bathroom door. Turning, she opened the shower door and adjusted the water temperature to her satisfaction. As soon as she stepped into the glass enclosure and began lathering her hair, she sighed with relief.

The hot water eased some of the tension in her neck and shoulders, and as she stood beneath the steamy spray, she wished her mind were as easily wiped clean. Yet the memory of a green-eyed weaver of dreams persisted, and her face wore a definite scowl by the time she rinsed and toweled herself dry.

Sharon dressed hurriedly, then sat cross-legged on her rumpled bed to blow-dry her hair. She usually found the warm flow of air soothing, but today she doubted if anything could calm her frazzled nerves. After replacing the dryer and brush in the bathroom cabinet, she twisted her luxuriant, slightly damp hair into a neat chignon, then began making her bed.

There was sand in the sheets, a visual reminder of last night. With a muttered imprecation she stripped the bed and stormed into the bathroom to dump the sheets in the hamper. When she returned she gathered clean sheets from the hall closet, then smoothed them impatiently over the mattress. She glared at the brown-and-tan quilted bedspread and gave the pillow shams in the same neat print an extra thump. No matter how hard she tried, she thought in disgust, she couldn't seem to forget a single magic moment of her meeting with Rob.

She left her apartment earlier than usual and began the long drive into Mill Valley. The mountain road wound in and out of green forest glades, and she gained a good deal of inner peace from her surroundings. She remembered Rob's words of friendship, as well as the look in his eyes that asked for so much more. By the time she arrived at her restaurant, Another Touch of Italy, she still hadn't decided whether or not she should see him again.

Sharon was in time to help serve brunch. She noticed that nearly every linen-draped table was filled, but instead of experiencing satisfaction she was annoyed. The constant hum of conversation increased her tension, and she couldn't seem to get her mind in working order.

Eventually she escaped into the privacy of her office, and the next few hours dragged by with annoying slowness. She forced herself to concentrate on her bookwork, getting the ledgers ready to show the accountant when he came on Tuesday. Last month Bill Harmon had asked her out and at the memory she pursed her lips in irritation. He was a nice enough man, but right now a night out with any member of the male sex wasn't on a list of her most favorite things to do. If he thought she needed him to spice up more than the books, he had another think coming!

It was four o'clock before Sharon closed the weekly ledger and carefully studied the profit and loss sheet for last month. After adding up the columns she double-checked to make certain her figures were correct. Even after expenses were met and salaries paid, she realized she would be left with a tidy profit. If she budgeted carefully, she thought, she would soon have enough saved to begin a catering service like the one she'd operated in partnership with Marilyn and Casey. Strangely enough the realization brought little pleasure. Was she fated to center her life around work? she wondered with a tired sigh.

There was more to life than operating a restaurant, no matter how successful it had proven to be. Wasn't it about time she adjusted her thinking accordingly? If she didn't she would end up with nothing but regrets. Some people could be contented with the outward trappings of success, but she wasn't one of them. There was a great emptiness inside of her that needed to be filled, and she was obsessed with the desire to reach outside of herself for that fulfillment.

Replacing the ledger in the bottom drawer of her desk, she left her office and went in search of her assistant. She found Claudia in the kitchen checking the contents of their cavernous walk-in freezer. Only four-foot-ten in her stocking feet, her salt-and-pepper hair cut short and a pair of granny glasses perched on the end of her nose, Sharon thought her friend and business manager looked like a skinny, lovable little pixie. "Claudia, can you handle things alone here tonight?"

The other woman turned. The frown wrinkling her brow made her appear more elfin than ever. "Is anything wrong, Sharon?"

The alarm in her voice was unmistakable, and Sharon smiled. She didn't have to wonder if Claudia viewed her as a workaholic, she thought in amusement. The surprised look on her face spoke for itself. "Everything's fine," she said. "I just feel like leaving early for a change."

"You never leave early," Claudia retorted, her eyes narrowing perceptively. "Do you want to talk about it?"

Sharon felt her cheeks become heated and quickly glanced away. "There's nothing to talk about," she muttered evasively. "Nothing at all!"

At what point Sharon made up her mind to return to the beach in search of Rob she couldn't have said. The decision might have been in her subconscious during the hours she worked in her office, feeling as though the walls were closing in around her. Or it could have been made during the drive home when she felt almost smothered by her own isolation. Whenever it happened, by the time Sharon arrived at her apartment, she was trembling with excitement.

She changed into jeans and a favorite yellow pullover sweater, aware of how well the color flattered her dark hair and eyes. Remembering how close she'd come to freezing the night before, she decided to carry rather than wear her lightweight windbreaker. She wanted to look her best when she met him again, and she hoped he wouldn't look too closely at the pair of battered but comfortable tennis shoes she slipped onto her feet.

As she neared the rock-strewn breakwater she marveled at the energy she still felt after walking such a distance. There was an elated spring to her steps and a feeling of anticipation caused her mouth to curl upward in a smile. Suddenly she felt young and confident, as though she would burst with the sheer joy of being alive. She was oblivious to the people she passed, her whole being concentrated on reaching her destination, and Rob.

Only an inner certainty told her she had found the right place. The sea had washed away every trace of the sandcastle, and Rob wasn't there to reassure her. With a growing feeling of apathy she stared down at a single shell abandoned by the tidewater, her thoughts filled with the mental image of herself and Rob kneeling together, side by side. Her involuntary sigh was a lonely sound on the still air.

"Hello, Princess."

With a murmur of relief Sharon turned, her emotions plainly written on her face. "I thought you wouldn't come."

"I was delayed," he muttered, his breath unsettled. "I was afraid I'd be too late."

Sharon didn't know who made the first sound, but suddenly they were both laughing uncontrollably. With a shout of elation Rob lifted her and swung her around in a circle. Her hands were braced on his shoulders as he stopped his dizzy spiraling, and his eyes glowed with a happiness that matched her own.

"Are you ready for the master castle builder to teach you his craft?" he asked as he lowered her to the ground.

His hands still lingered against her waist, and Sharon felt their imprint through her clothes. The sensation was as arousing as if she were naked, and the laughter left her eyes. She stepped away from him, her expression setting unspoken boundaries. "I'm ready for my friend to teach me how to build sandcastles."

Rob's features sobered as he leaned toward her and reached for her hand. "Amendment duly noted and recorded in my brain, my friend."

Even though he seemed reluctant to release her fingers, she was reassured by the sincerity in his voice. With a carefree laugh she pulled away from his warm clasp and tilted her head back to savor the scent of the sea. The restlessness she'd been trying to ignore for most of the day appeared somehow magnified by Rob's presence, and she knew she was too tense to remain still for an extended period of time. "Rob, would you be disappointed if we gave our building efforts a miss this evening?"

The eyes that met hers were questioning and oddly wary. "Do you have to leave?"

"Of course not. I'm just too keyed up to stay in one place for very long." She grinned at his relieved expression and gave a rueful shrug of her shoulders. "I have the strangest urge to jump around. Do you think the princess is turning into a frog?"

He tilted his head and considered her with mocking seriousness. "Maybe I should kiss you just in case."

His voice held a teasing inflection as he reached for her, and yet there was a poignant expression in the depths of his eyes that caught at Sharon's breath. She agilely dodged his outflung arms. "Wait a minute," she said as she continued to retreat from his stalking figure. "Since you're not a prince, a kiss from you wouldn't do me any good. That would make you my brother, remember?"

Rob smacked the heel of his palm against his forehead and grinned at her when she winced. "Then I'll be the frog, and you can kiss me."

Sharon bunched her hands on her hips and tried to control the leaping pulse caused by his suggestion. "I think we'd better switch fairy tales before we get into trouble."

He laughed, noticing the militant sparkle in her eyes, then raised his arms in a gesture of surrender. "You can't switch fairy tales in midstream. It isn't proper."

"Who says I have to be proper?"

The laughter in his eyes was replaced by an emotion far more disturbing. "You can be improper with me anytime, Sharon."

Sharon could have cut out her tongue, but it was far too late to retract her thoughtless words. With a disgruntled mutter she folded her arms across her chest and gave him a baleful stare. "You're making me mad, Frog!"

"All right," he conceded with a grin, "Will you forgive me if I buy you a hamburger?"

Sharon's arms dropped to her sides, and she arched her brow in inquiry. "How did you know I was hungry?"

He guided her across the sand, reaching for her hand to pull her up on the breakwater embankment.

"Where you're concerned I must be psychic," he said, turning his head to look at her as she walked by his side. "I'm an ambitious man, Sharon. One of these days I'm going to know you better than you do yourself, so be warned."

Sharon dismissed his warning as they passed through a graveled alley between privately owned properties and walked the short distance to the center of town. As they approached she studied the buildings that comprised Stinson Beach. To refer to the two rows of wooden structures bisected by a pitted asphalt road as a town was a misnomer. There were several shops which catered to tourists, a small grocery store, a couple of dilapidated gasoline pumps and a restaurant that also served as a bar. It wasn't a thriving metropolis and that was why Sharon liked it so much. She wouldn't have changed a thing. She said as much to Rob as they stepped onto the sidewalk and entered the restaurant whose design was reminiscent of the old west.

He nodded his agreement. "I feel the same."

He seated her at one of the round wooden tables and glanced at their surroundings as he lowered himself into a chair across from her. "This place has an air of timelessness about it. Sometimes I come here in the evenings for a beer and sit at the bar imagining I'm a modern-day Rip Van Winkle. I find myself wondering what would happen if I fell asleep for twenty years."

Sharon stared across the short distance separating them, fascinated by the play of emotions on Rob's face. She felt as though she were being gently guided into a realm of imagination she'd never experienced in her own childhood. The harsh realities of life had touched her before she'd had a chance to enjoy her youth. She was saddened by the thought. "I wish I could be more like you, Rob."

His gaze captured the wistfulness of her expression. "In what way?"

She lowered her eyes to the red-and-white checked tablecloth and traced the surface with her finger. "I don't know," she admitted quietly. "Maybe I'm envious of your ability to relax and enjoy yourself."

He braced his elbows on the table and rested his chin on his interlocking fingers. "When did you stop enjoying life, Sharon?"

Her head jerked up, and she looked at him with startled eyes. She wanted to answer his question with a denial, but found herself unable to utter a word. How could she return his honesty with a lie? "Is that what's wrong with me, Rob?"

"There's nothing wrong with you," he said, his strong features softened with gentleness. "You've just forgotten how to play."

The simplicity of his remark caused an emotional lump to lodge in her throat, and her voice sounded shaken as she asked, "Will you help me to remember?"

His lowered glance caught the slight trembling of her lips and his own curved in a smile. "What are friends for, Princess?"

She laughed unsteadily. "I might be a terrible pupil."

"I'll take a chance on you."

The waitress arrived at their table, her eyes dreamy as she ogled Rob. He played up to her shamefully. By the time the young girl noticed someone else seated at the table, Sharon had trouble pushing words past the laughter building in her chest. "You should be ashamed of yourself," she choked, her eyes following the exaggerated sway of feminine hips as the waitress disappeared into the kitchen.

"Lesson Number One in how to play," he intoned stentoriously. "The pupil never tells the teacher he should be ashamed of himself."

"Why not?"

His assumed arrogance turned into a grin. "Because he says so."

"That's not fair!"

"I don't have to be fair," he countered with open satisfaction. "I'm the teacher and anything that makes you laugh is okay to have on the curriculum."

"You make me laugh," she said, putting action to words.

He gave a regal nod of his head and then ruined the effect by leering at her. "It's okay to have me too, sweetness."

"It is not!" she gasped, glad the dimness of the room hid her blush.

"Hey, who's the teacher around here?"

She gave him a warning glance. "Just as long as you remember to stay on the subject."

He gave a disgruntled sigh, his eyes mournful as he looked at her. "Sex education was always my best subject in school."

Sharon hadn't intended to do more than sip from her water glass, but as Rob spoke she gulped more than she was prepared to swallow. He jumped up and began patting her on the back. When she finally got her breath back she glared up at him and said, "I'll just bet it was!"

The waitress returned with their food. She served Sharon first before turning to place Rob's hamburger in front of him. The sultry glance the waitress gave Rob made Sharon want to poke her with a fork, but when Rob merely thanked her politely Sharon managed to resist temptation. Yet she couldn't prevent the satisfied smile that curved her mouth as she began to eat, anymore than she could help being pleased at the disappointment in the other woman's eyes.

Sharon's restlessness had disappeared by the time they finished eating. The plates had been removed, their coffee cups refilled and still they lingered to enjoy each other's company. She felt completely relaxed with him, and she was amazed by the realization. Not since Michael had she felt so contented in the company of a man, and she found the knowledge puzzling.

Physically there were few similarities between the two men. Where Michael had been lean and lanky, Rob was exceptionally muscled. He was also the taller of the two, and his thick blond hair, full and brushing the back of his collar, didn't bear the slightest resemblance to the bright red regulation crew cut Michael had worn. Yet there was something about Rob that was hauntingly familiar, and her eyes followed him as he walked over to the bar to pay for their meal.

While Rob waited beside the cash register, he turned to smile at her, and she caught her breath as full awareness flooded her being. Michael's smile had been as sweetly tender as Rob's, she thought, trying to repress a vicious stab of bitterness. His blue eyes had shone with his faith in tomorrow and had been as boldly confident as the green eyes that watched her from across the room. Yet for Michael there had been no tomorrows, and she had been left with only yesterday's dreams.

At that thought something inside Sharon broke apart and reformed. She felt curiously empty, and as she left the restaurant at Rob's side, she remembered the promise she'd made on the day Michael was buried. She had gazed out at an endless sea of identical white crosses, aching to have his final resting place stand out from all the others.

It was then that she had vowed always to keep Michael alive in her heart. She'd kept her promise to him, she thought, and yet in doing so she had built a wall around her heart. The emotional barrier kept her safe from pain, even if the price she paid meant shutting herself away from the kind of happiness she had known with Michael.

That was the similarity between the two men she had sensed from the beginning. They both approached life with a lighthearted confidence she couldn't share. Her shy, introverted nature had been drawn to Michael the way she was drawn to Rob, and she was frightened by the comparison. Rob didn't quite fit the role of friend and something inside of her recoiled from the thought.

"Sharon, what's wrong?"

She was jolted from her introspection by the sound of Rob's voice. They were following a dusty path that led down to the beach, and when she glanced up at him she saw a troubled look in his eyes. Forcing herself to smile, she shrugged. "Nothing's wrong, Rob."

His hand on her arm halted her progress. "You haven't spoken since we left the restaurant," he said, his frustration plain as he noticed her guarded expression. "Have I said or done anything to upset you?"

She fought down an urge to tell him her thoughts were her own. She wanted to tell him that he had no right to penetrate the part of herself she kept hidden. But when his hands settled on her shoulders, she couldn't prevent herself from responding to the gentleness of his touch. A warm rush of affection for him eased some of the coldness she felt inside and this time the smile she gave him reached her eyes. "You're not to blame for my rotten mood. I'm sorry if I—"

"You have nothing to be sorry for," he interrupted with quiet firmness, "unless it's trying to hide the way you really feel from me."

She flinched inwardly from the pain she saw in his eyes. "It's difficult for me to talk about my feelings with anyone, Rob. I've enjoyed your company very much, and I certainly never meant you to feel slighted by my behavior."

He shook his head, and his features hardened as he looked at her. "I don't need a polite little speech to pacify my wounded ego, Sharon."

She stiffened and gazed back at him with visible impatience. "Then what do you want from me, Rob?"

"Just be yourself and don't place reservations on our relationship. There should be truth between friends."

"We've known each other such a short time," she said, her brow creased in a frown. "Why is my friendship so important to you?"

"Because I sense you're special, Sharon. You're sensitive and caring, and your eyes hold a basic integrity I admire deeply. I'm so tired of playing games, of indulging in surface relationships devoid of honesty."

Her eyes held startled awareness. "You've been hurt badly in the past, haven't you?"

Rob didn't try to evade her scrutiny. He met her questioning gaze openly and looked pleased by the concern in her dark eyes. "Yes, honey. Like you, I'm no stranger to pain."

"You don't have to talk about it if you don't want to."

"There isn't much to tell," he said quietly. "I was young and idealistic and infatuated with a student at the university I attended. She had a way of looking at a man..." He paused, shaking his head as if to clear it of a remembered presence. "Anyway, when she told me she loved me I felt about ten feet tall. I went around in a delirious daze of happiness until a friend of mine told me she was playing me for a fool. I discovered the truth for myself when I came home unexpectedly one afternoon and found her in bed with one of the jocks from the football team."

"I'm sorry, Rob."

He smiled at Sharon's distressed expression. "I was sorry enough for myself," he admitted wryly. "I'm afraid the experience made me cynical where the female sex was concerned."

Sharon tilted her head and studied his features. "You don't seem cynical to me."

"Because you're different, Sharon. That's why I want only truth between us, not lies presented under the guise of politeness. I want you to be yourself, not someone acting a role because you think it's expected of you."

She lowered her eyes to his chest. "I value your friendship too, Rob, but I'm a private person. I can't change the way I am to please you."

"You don't have to confide in me, but when you're miserable you sure as hell don't have to plaster a smile on your face for my benefit."

Her head lifted, and the grin that curved her mouth wasn't for his benefit...it was for her own. "Do you know what I've suddenly realized about you, Rob?"

"I may be crazy, but I'm going to risk another bruise to my tender ego," he said with a laugh. "What have you found out about me, honey?"

"Your ego is safe," she said teasingly. "I've simply decided it's impossible to stay miserable around you for long. Sandcastle men must have a special magic all their own."

"Speaking of sandcastles, we never did get around to building ours," he said, gesturing with rueful emphasis toward the setting sun. "Since tomorrow is Sunday, would you be able to spend the day with me?"

Sharon considered the tempting prospect of an entire day spent in Rob's company. Tomorrow the restaurant was only open for lunch, she thought, but Sundays were usually quite busy. She knew she should be there to help Claudia, but as she saw the eager light in Rob's eyes begin to fade she threw responsibility aside for the first time in her life. "I'd love to spend Sunday with you, Rob."

Three

────────

The April weather was kind during the days that followed. The skies were blue and cloudless, the wind off the water brisk but not chill. Sharon arranged for Claudia to take over the operation of the restaurant in the evenings, which left her free to meet Rob. Claudia was bursting with curiosity, but seemed to sense her employer's need for privacy, although she often watched Sharon with a worried expression on her face.

Sharon would have liked to ease Claudia's mind, but she had to keep the knowledge of Rob's existence to herself. She knew she was acting out of character, but she really didn't care. The hours spent with Rob became more special as the week drew to a close, and she had an almost superstitious dread of something occurring to spoil their friendship. She wanted to continue living a fantasy existence for as long as possible and talking about Rob to anyone else might break the spell she was under.

A phone call from her sister was the catalyst that caused a serious threat to Sharon's happiness. She was in her office when she took the call, her hand tightening on the receiver when she realized Marilyn was crying.

"Marilyn, try to calm yourself," she pleaded. "I can't understand you."

Sharon heard her sister muffle a sob, which was accompanied by an audibly indrawn breath. "Papa's been admitted to the hospital, Sharon. He's having chest pains."

"Dear God," Sharon murmured, closing her eyes in an effort to cling to her self-control. "How bad, Marilyn?"

"I drove him here and he was doubled over," she replied stiltedly. "I . . . he acted like he might be having a heart attack."

"Have you called Paul and Eric?"

There was the sound of a sniff and finally Marilyn said, "They're on their way here now. Oh, Sharon, what if Papa—"

"Don't say it," Sharon interrupted, her calm manner belied by the paleness of her face. She glanced up and saw Claudia hovering in the doorway. Gesturing the other woman forward, she then tried to give her sister the reassurance she needed badly herself. "Try to stay calm until I get there, Marilyn."

"Yes, but come as quickly as you can," Marilyn begged, her voice on the edge of hysteria. "I'm so scared, Sharon."

"I'm leaving now," she said gently. "Everything will be all right, *piccola*."

Sharon's words proved prophetic. Her father's condition was much improved by the time she arrived at the hospital. She entered his room to find him sitting up in bed as hearty and boisterous as ever. She nearly crumpled with relief and raised questioning brows at Marilyn. Her sister smiled and moved forward to hug her. "They've ruled out a heart attack."

Sharon bent down to kiss her father and murmured, "Must you always do everything with such fervor, Papa? I aged ten years on the drive over here."

Paulo Vecchio's booming laugh rang out as he returned his daughter's embrace. "I do everything with gusto, eh?"

Sharon grinned at him and glanced at her brothers. "Has anyone talked with the doctor?"

Paul nodded. "You should have heard Papa roar when Dr. Stanley accused him of eating too much pasta."

"I have the iron stomach," their father protested, remembered ire in his brown eyes.

"You might have an iron stomach," Sharon said, "but you weren't in that much pain for nothing!"

"Ahhh, always my sensible angel."

Sharon shook her head, and looked down at him with a smirk. "You aren't going to get around me that easily, Papa. Just what did you have for dinner?"

Paulo gazed sheepishly at his eldest offspring. "Well, maybe the fettuccine wasn't cooked properly."

Marilyn stepped forward, her stance indignant. "Might I remind you that I was the one who cooked that fettuccine?"

Paulo's eyes sparkled with glee, yet he glanced around the room with a mournful expression. "Ahhh, how a father suffers for his children!"

"It wasn't the fettuccine, Paulo."

The Vecchio family turned laughing eyes toward the doctor, who entered the room after first offering a brief greeting to the visitors. He approached his patient with the ease of a friend of long standing, slapping a chart against the side of the bed. "You have gallstones."

"I have what?"

Unfazed by her father's enraged reaction, Sharon stepped forward. "Will he have to undergo surgery, Dr. Stanley?"

The elderly man shook his head and favored them all with a smile. He ignored his irascible patient. "The condition isn't advanced, and it won't be if you can get this cantankerous Italian to stick to a diet."

While preparing for bed that night Sharon remembered her father's reaction to the doctor's advice. She smiled into the darkness, confident that Paulo Vecchio would follow the doctor's orders. If he didn't, Marilyn had threatened to move in with him. Sharon chuckled to herself as she pictured her father's reaction to Marilyn's words. Paulo had immediately stopped blustering.

Sharon's last thought before falling asleep was of Rob. She'd missed her rendezvous with the sandcastle man.

Sharon hurried across the sand toward a tall figure who was pacing back and forth like a prowling lion. She thought how apt the simile was when his thick golden mane of hair was tossed by the wind. There was a smile on her face, and he turned at the sound of her approach. "Hello, Rob."

In two strides he was before her, a tenseness in his muscular body that Sharon found difficult to ignore. "What happened to you last night?"

"I'm sorry," she said, pausing to catch her breath. "I was unavoidably detained."

"Is that the only explanation I'm going to get?" he questioned angrily, brushing his tumbled hair from his forehead in exasperation.

Sharon's chin tilted aggressively. "And if it is?"

Rob heard the hurt underlying her words and his expression softened. "I was frightened, Sharon."

He saw the tears flooding her eyes, and with a gentleness that left her whole body trembling, he drew her into his arms. He began to kiss away her tears, and Sharon's heart thundered against the wall of her chest.

Being held by him felt so good, she thought, and with unconscious yearning she wrapped her arms around his neck. Their bodies touched and seemed to cling together as Rob's mouth captured hers in a groan of pleasure.

There was no beginning and no end to what they were feeling. As the kiss ended and their eyes met, both of their faces reflected the startled wonder triggered by their embrace. Neither questioned the rightness of the moment. They began to walk slowly, and Sharon described the events of the previous evening to Rob. His arm tightened around her waist and his eyes held an embarrassed gleam as he met her candid gaze.

"I'm afraid my imagination got the better of me," he admitted with a grimace. "I'm sorry I let my temper loose on you."

They stopped walking, and with a gesture of forgiveness Sharon stepped forward to hug him. "I didn't know you even had a temper."

"I'm usually cool and collected, but I felt so damn helpless last night, Sharon."

"I know," she whispered, leaning back to look at him. "I didn't mean to worry you. I'm sorry, Rob."

He gazed into her eyes, and the world stood still. Slowly his head descended. With a tiny cry of need Sharon responded to the mouth that plundered the sweetness of her lips. There was hunger in his kiss, but there was also a desperation that met its match in her. There was no thought of denial as she felt his hands convulsively stroke her arched back and the swell of her hips. At that moment they were two people who were no longer alone.

"Don't ask me to apologize for that kiss," he groaned, his hand brushing the hair back from her flushed cheek. "I want you, Sharon."

Sharon's breath was suspended in her chest as she read the message in his eyes. Her heart took up the thundering beat of the ocean pounding against the shore as she responded to his unspoken question. Her hands stroked his hair as he pressed his mouth against her throat.

"I know," she whispered unevenly.

Sharon and Rob smiled at each other as they turned to continue their walk. The arm he rested across her shoulders kept her tucked firmly by his side, and her hand clasped his waist as she realized there was nowhere else she'd rather be. She felt safe and sheltered by his body, her emotions spiraling with a sense of euphoria she didn't stop to question.

"Have you had dinner?"

Sharon shook her head, her voice amused as she admitted, "I was in too much of a hurry to get here."

"Does the idea of coming home with me to share an omelet seem out of place?"

"No," she murmured shyly, silently berating herself for her monosyllabic reply. She was almost thirty years old, she thought with growing frustration, of sound mind, and about as sophisticated in a situation like this as a gawky teenager. She didn't think Rob had dinner on his mind anymore than she did. There was a sensual current flowing between them that needed no verbal acknowledgment . . . only acceptance.

Firming her mouth resolutely in preparation for what she was about to say, Sharon lifted her head and met his eyes. The compassionate understanding reflected in his emerald gaze caught her by surprise. "You know I've never done anything like this, don't you?"

He looked at her, and she stiffened in amazed comprehension. As though sensing her need for reassurance, his grin tilted in a teasing slant. "You've never accepted an invitation to dinner? Are all the men you've known blind, or just certifiable idiots?"

Sharon couldn't make herself smile. Her body was rigid with tension as she asked, "Is dinner with a friend all you expect?"

"No."

Just one word spoken in a temperate tone of voice, and yet his honesty hit her with the force of a blow. She heard her breathing grow harsh and felt an embarrassing tide of color flush her skin with heat. With awkward clumsiness she turned her back to him. She gave forth one gigantic prayer, hoping the ground would split apart in one of California's famous earthquakes and swallow her whole.

She wasn't lucky enough to have her wish granted. She was still standing paralyzed in place when his hands moved to cup her shoulders. She felt the warmth of his breath against her hair as he exhaled forcibly. "You deserve more than a lie from me, Sharon."

She squeezed her eyes tightly shut. "It's just that I—"

"It's all right, I understand."

She tilted her head back to look at him. "Do you?"

He nodded and touched her mouth with caressing fingers. "I'm taking our friendship farther than you'd intended, but you don't have to worry. We all do things on impulse sometimes, but that doesn't necessarily mean they're wrong. You asked me if I expected more from you than dinner, and I gave you as truthful an answer as I'm capable of." He sighed and rubbed his thumb against the curve of her jaw. "I can't tell you that I don't want you in my bed. After what just happened between us you know that isn't true. I've spent every hour since we met wondering what it would be like to make love to you, and I'm not ashamed of those thoughts. Afraid, maybe. But not ashamed."

"Afraid?"

He smiled at her startled expression. "Do you think only women suffer from a fear of inadequacy? Men are expected to make all the moves, and that in itself can be as frightening as hell."

"But you're so self-assured."

His mouth twisted wryly. "I might have viewed the female populace with cynicism, but I've been around, honey. Hell, any normal man pushing forty has had his share of experience, but the women I've been in-

volved with have known the score from the beginning. I've asked no questions and made no promises.
When a relationship ended I walked away without regrets. Until now that was all I expected from a woman.
With you I want more, Sharon.''

"You wanted a friend," she interrupted, his words
alarming her.

"I'll settle for friendship," he said, his eyes tender
as they studied her confusion. "For now I'll be satisfied just to learn what makes you happy and to comfort you when you're sad. I want to explore your
mind, and when the time is right for both of us, I want
to explore your body. I won't ask for more than you're
willing to give—that I promise you. Tonight we'll
share an omelet, a glass of wine and some conversation. Anything else will be up to you, all right?''

Sharon's tense frame relaxed until she was resting
against him, and she twisted her head around to show
him a relieved smile. "Can I have a glass of milk instead of wine?''

His deep chuckle ended on a pleased shout, and he
hugged her exuberantly. "You can have anything you
want, Princess.''

Rob's home came as a complete surprise. Like
Sharon, he lived within walking distance of the beach,
but there all similarity ended. Her apartment was a
comfortable, if rather small, one-bedroom unit. Rob's
cottage stood only a few yards from the sand, almost
hidden by a huge, twisted cypress. There were other

homes nearby, but somehow his little house looked lonely and forlorn. The elements had not been kind to the weathered wood surrounding its sagging frame and had left behind an inheritance of frailty in the small structure.

"What are you thinking?"

Sharon stood in the center of the cottage. If she moved one step in either direction she was afraid she'd find herself outside. The walls were of knotty pine, and a large beam slashed across the center of the structure like a giant exclamation point. Besides the front door, there were two other doors, which she presumed led to Rob's bedroom and a bathroom. Between the doors was a long divan, and her fingers itched to straighten the large bolster pillows leaning drunkenly against the wall.

She had shaken the sand out of her shoes before entering, leaving them outside on the sagging porch. Now, as her toes curled into the colorfully patterned Navaho rug that covered the center of the pitted wooden floor, she tried to think of a polite answer to Rob's question. "It's very...cozy," she finally managed.

His eyes sparkled wickedly as he gestured toward the postage-sized kitchenette. "The kitchen's small but labor-saving."

There was a battered white refrigerator in the corner, a two-burner gas stove and a chipped enamel sink. To the left was a plain wooden table with two straight-backed chairs. Sharon glanced at Rob with suspicion, but his expression remained bland. It might be labor-saving, she thought, but whoever had painted those cupboards that bilious green color needed his head examined. She only hoped the artist hadn't been Rob. "Uh, that rock fireplace is lovely."

She'd turned her back on the kitchen and Rob in desperation, her eyes focusing on the only attractive feature the cottage boasted. Covering the entire wall, the fireplace had been formed of large pieces of rust-veined rock in variegated earthen tones. She concentrated intently on the wide opening as she heard Rob approach her from behind.

"Is there something wrong?"

Sharon frowned, certain she had heard his voice shake as he questioned her. Turning slowly, she asked, "Is that the bathroom?"

She pointed to one of the doors that had first caught her attention. Rob nodded his head. At this she smiled brightly. "At least you have indoor plumbing!"

With a shout of laughter he swooped forward and grabbed her in a bear hug that threatened to crack every bone in her body. Her face was crushed against his chest, and his chocolate brown sweater tickled her nose until she sneezed. At this his hold loosened, and his hilarity subsided into husky chuckles. Keeping his hands on her shoulders, he stepped back, then surveyed her indignant expression, not even trying to hide the humor in his own.

"You, my lady, are priceless!"

Her chin took on a belligerent tilt. "Well, the fireplace is lovely."

"Of course it is."

"And the cottage is very clean," she said with increased exasperation.

"Ummm, and I have the callouses to prove it."

"You will also," she breathed warningly, "have an accompanying lump on your head if you don't stop teasing me."

He threw up his hands in mock surrender and grinned at her. "Has getting riled increased your appetite?"

Her petulant expression changed to one of sheepishness. "I'm starving!"

They fixed their meal together and talked nonstop as they worked. After they'd eaten they shared cleanup duties, and Sharon heard Rob's plans to renovate the cottage. When she realized only the rock wall would remain intact, her original antipathy toward the old building was abruptly reversed. As darkness fell the room took on an air of serenity. Soft lamplight cast friendly shadows on the walls, and the glow and crackle of the fire Rob had started added to her contentment.

They enjoyed their coffee in front of the fireplace, seating themselves on the hand-braided rug and leaning back against the bolster pillows Rob had removed from the divan. As she finished the last swallow of her drink, Sharon sighed with unfeigned satisfaction, feeling as though she were living a dream as she stared at the leaping flames with bemused attention. When Rob rose on one elbow, blocking her view of the fire with his body, the thought of moving briefly entered Sharon's mind, but was quickly discarded.

Slowly her hand reached up to trace the contours of his smiling lips, which opened to allow further exploration. With growing fascination she felt the smooth, even edges of his strong white teeth nibble at her marauding finger, hearing the increasingly rapid flow of his breath as his tongue began its own provoking search. Each of her fingers were tasted with delicate thoroughness, and her eyes closed to savor the sensations now tingling against her open palm.

"Look at me, honey."

Sharon did as he asked, her thick lashes flickering against her cheeks before they lifted to expose her innermost thoughts to his questioning gaze. Her lids felt heavy, and she knew he could easily read the desire she felt for him in her eyes. As though they had a mind of their own her hands sought the back of his head. Her fingers buried themselves in the thick, wavy strands of lustrous gold that brushed the edge of his crew-necked sweater.

With a groan Rob's mouth lowered to her throat, his voice muffled as he asked, "Is now the right time for us, love?"

Sharon's lashes fluttered in a shy attempt to hide the intensity of her response from him. She was trembling with a need too strong to deny, her body aching for the release she knew could be found in his arms.

She tried to tell herself she barely knew this man, and yet with every atom of her being she realized such unemotional logic was wrong. He was no stranger, she thought. He was part of the puzzle that would make her whole, and she wanted him with a desperation that shocked her into giving him the answer he sought.

Her timidly whispered affirmative was swallowed by his hungrily foraging mouth. His hands cupped her flushed cheeks, their warmth adding to the fire blazing out of control inside her body. Her back arched, and she shuddered as the hardening outline of his body settled against her welcoming softness. When his weight bore her back against the pillows, she instinctively responded to the compelling thrust of his hips.

The warmth of his lips blazed across her mouth, and her senses were overwhelmed by the taste of him. As her churning emotions rose, her hands began to memorize his shape. The clothes that formed a barrier between them soon became an unbearable irritant.

As though he, too, resented the material that prevented their bodies from closer contact, Rob lifted her sweater over her head. She watched his hands as he undressed her, and a surge of tenderness made her feel dizzy when she realized how badly his hands were shaking. Gone was the man in control, and in his place was an aroused male who made no effort to hide from her eyes what he was feeling.

His honesty could only be met with her own. Moistening her kiss-stung lips with the tip of her tongue, Sharon began to tug at Rob's clothing. Every inch of bronzed skin that was revealed as his garments dropped to the floor became her reward, and within minutes they were each enjoying unrestricted freedom.

Sharon's thoughts spun as her hands began a journey of exploration. Encouraged by Rob's broken murmurs of pleasure, her moist palms absorbed the heat of his body. His masculine beauty slowly imprinted itself on her mind—the memory of smooth hard angles and crisp golden hair trapped forever inside of her head.

Rob seemed to sense Sharon's need to climb slowly toward the highest pinnacles of sensation, and he exhibited a torturous degree of self-control. But soon his patience was overcome by desire and passivity gave way to the demands of his body. His yearning mouth fed itself on the taste and texture of her, and his hands began their own path of exploration.

By touch he discovered the heaviness of her full breasts, while his tongue bathed the tumescent crests until she cried out. Encouraged by her whimpers of pleasure he continued his intimate study of her body, and the lips that nibbled a trail of fire across her hips found a resting place against her stomach. He planted slow kisses on the soft curves he found there, while his fingers discovered her molten core.

Again she cried out and arched her hips to meet his searching fingers. Rob's reassuring murmur was lost as he resisted her shocked attempt to move away from his exquisitely tempting mouth. After endless minutes he could no longer delay his own fulfillment. Sharon's arms drew him to her as he gently entered her with a hoarse cry.

In that instant Sharon, too, experienced the full power of her womanhood. As she opened herself to the surge of raw vitality Rob exuded, she trapped the very essence of his masculine strength inside of her body. He was held by her warmth and as he strove for completion, he carried her with him.

Higher and higher they rose, clinging together until their individual strength merged into a force so powerful their bodies exploded in unrestrained delight. When each subsided into an aftermath of contentment, they gave in to the rest their bodies craved. They sought the deep sleep of satiation still wrapped tightly within each other's arms.

Four

Sharon awoke in the early hours of the morning. When she first lifted her eyelids she frowned groggily, uncertain of her surroundings. Narrowing her eyes to focus her gaze, her attention was caught by a pair of jeans draped carelessly over a straight-backed chair in the far corner of the shadowed room. They were wide and long and by no stretch of the imagination would they ever fit someone of her diminutive size!

As she stared at the jeans her memory sharpened. Her eyes widened in disbelief. Had the sensual woman of last night really been shy, emotionally repressed Sharon Vecchio? Had she really made love with a man she had known for such a short time? Cautiously she turned her head, and there on the pillow next to her was the evidence she sought.

Rob's breathing was deep and even and sleep had softened his features. He lay on his side facing her, with the sheet and blanket bunched around his waist. As though he'd gotten warm during the night, he'd kicked one leg free of the covers. Sharon's gaze traveled from a well-formed foot to a muscular thigh. Her breathing quickened as she pictured the male perfection hidden from her view. Hurriedly she lifted her eyes, her attention caught by his hair, tousled strands of a pure gold color against the white pillowcase.

Becoming fully roused, Sharon finally remembered being carried into Rob's bedroom. Just the thought of him holding her naked body while she remained half asleep caused her to shudder with embarrassment. She felt exposed and vulnerable, as though the happenings of last night had somehow changed her. The lovemaking she and Rob had indulged in had left its mark. Her body ached in unfamiliar places as did her heart. So much for the innocent friendship that had begun to mean so much to her, she thought sadly. Now they were lovers, and Rob would expect the change to be permanent. What else could he think?

She remembered the words he'd spoken to her...was it a hundred years ago? *Tonight we'll share an omelet, a glass of wine and some conversation. Anything else will be up to you.* Well, Sharon, she thought with a grimace of distaste, you certainly grabbed hold of "anything else" with a vengeance! She'd acted like a sex-starved old maid, and she deserved Rob's contempt as well as her own.

Tears of humiliation flooded her eyes, and yet she refused to indulge in a good old-fashioned crying jag. To do so might give her a little relief, but it wouldn't do much for her self-esteem. Strangely enough, resuming her inspection of Rob calmed her. As had happened before, once her attention was focused on him she couldn't make herself look away.

Sharon became fascinated by Rob's face, composed and boyishly innocent as he slept. His mouth was slightly parted, and enviously long, thick lashes formed crescent shadows against his high cheekbones.

Suddenly she recalled another face and her chest tightened with emotion. Pressing her mouth against her pillow to muffle a sob, she thought of the first morning she had awakened in Michael's arms. Then she hadn't felt any shame. She and Michael had known each other for months before they had gone to bed together, and the physical expression of their love had seemed so very right.

He had been gentle and kind, and she would never have thought the pleasure they experienced was lacking in any way. Yet last night had been a revelation. With Michael, a man she'd loved with all of her heart, lovemaking had been as serene as a lazily flowing river. With Rob, a man she hadn't known long enough to be sure how she felt about him, lovemaking had been a tempest of unparalleled sensation.

Betrayal! That was the most descriptive word she could think of when she remembered what she and Michael had had together. Last night had been betrayal of the past and of the contentment she'd known in the embrace of the only man she'd ever loved. Rob's passion had seared across her flesh and burned a path through her. She had never before experienced such a torrent of gratification, and the knowledge of her total response as a woman forever changed her from the innocent girl Michael had loved.

The thought didn't bring about the agony of loss she expected, and Sharon felt the bite of guilt tearing at her. She was adrift, cast out from the protection of the past with a brutal suddenness with which she couldn't begin to cope. She needed time to come to terms with what she felt for Rob...time to decide if what she felt for him was real, or merely a figment of her lonely imagination.

Her heart pounding a rhythm of nervousness against her chest, Sharon slipped quietly from the bed. Rob had thoughtfully brought her clothes in from the other room, and they were neatly folded on the seat of the same chair as his jeans. She found the sight of their clothing so close together oddly shocking. She clamped her hand over her mouth before she released the mocking laughter threatening to engulf her. The foolishness of her reasoning after the intimacies they had indulged in during the night made her wonder if she was entirely sane.

The wind gusted through the single, undraped window on the far side of the room, and she held her breath as she looked back at the bed. When Rob didn't stir, she exhaled a sigh of relief. With clumsy stealth she collected her things and tiptoed toward the door. She twisted the knob slowly, wincing as the scarred wooden panel squeaked open.

Last night's fire was just cold embers as she stepped into the living room and carefully closed the door behind her. There was no warmth coming from the rock-lined hearth, and every inch of Sharon's skin was covered with goose bumps by the time she finished dressing. The shadows in the room were quickly dispersing as the sun rose higher in the sky, and she turned her head so she wouldn't have to look at the bolster pillows still sprawled on top of the Navaho rug.

She didn't want to be reminded of what had happened last night, yet she soon discovered the memories were not easily erased. Even after she stepped out onto the porch and knelt to put on her shoes, she could still visualize Rob's broad shoulders, which had risen above her as they had lain together in front of the fire.

As she remembered how his gleaming, sun-kissed skin had blocked the heat from the fire, she trembled in the fog-dampened chill of early morning. She could still almost feel the imprint of his body upon hers.

Sharon didn't look back at the whimsically tilted little house, and yet she could remember every detail of its battered shape as she hurried toward the safety of her apartment. It had survived the ravages of time, but not without scars. Unlike her, she bitterly reflected, knowing the scars she carried were not visible to the naked eye. "Oh, Michael, I'm sorry," she whispered with an agonizing surge of remorse. "I'm so very sorry."

Sharon locked the wrought iron gate behind her as she stepped into the courtyard. Even as she secured the lock, her trembling fingers clumsy against the rusty metal, she acknowledged her cowardice. She only wished she could shut off her memory as easily as she could block off her access to the beach. But her mind refused to shelter her from her thoughts. Each detail of the night was replayed endlessly, a haunting refrain that served only to increase her heartache.

When a shower failed to release the tension that was causing a painful throbbing in her skull, Sharon opened herself to her memories. She felt again the touch of gentle hands and heard the encouraging whispers from a voice husky with barely restrained passion. All of her senses had come to life because of Rob's careful tutelage, and Sharon knew forgetting was impossible.

After hurriedly patting herself dry, Sharon dropped the towel in the hamper with a grimace of disgust. As she stepped into her bedroom, she determined not to waste another moment indulging in useless recriminations. She had a business to run and a hundred and one things to do before the day was over. First on her list was a drive into San Francisco to order provisions for the restaurant. There would be several stops to make, since the last delivery order from the meat-packing company had been used sooner than expected.

Sharon silently gave thanks that business was good, knowing if she kept herself busy enough she wouldn't have time to brood. She would place a larger beef order this time and then drive across town to Fisherman's Wharf to place a similar order for fresh seafood. Just mentally planning such familiar tasks gave her a sense of reprieve, and she walked toward her closet with an eagerness she didn't have to question. She needed to escape from her apartment where the sound of the sea against the shore outside was too vivid a reminder of fantasy castles and magic moments in a stranger's arms.

"Auntie Sharon, Auntie Sharon!"

A small, energy-packed body wearing a bright red swimsuit leaped into the air. Sharon caught him in mid-lunge, and her arms tightened into an enthusiastic hug. As his brown eyes searched her features, his expression was one of expectancy. With the ease of long practice Sharon bounced him in her arms, exhaling loudly in protest of his weight. "Jonathan, are you growing again?"

He giggled and nodded enthusiastically. "Uh, huh!"

She frowned ferociously as she continued the ritual of greeting her best friend's son. "You mean you kept growing after I told you to stop?"

The mock disapproval in her growling tones caused Jonathan to squirm with pleasure. "Course I did, Auntie Sharon," he declared proudly, wrapping his arms around her neck for another hug before he leaned back to look at her. "I'm getting bigger and bigger and—"

"I think Auntie Sharon has gotten the message, Jon."

At the inflection in Casey's voice Sharon turned toward her friend and grinned. "If your son doesn't stop growing so fast, he'll soon be carrying me around."

"I've already threatened to make him wear short pants," Casey declared with a teasing glance at her son. "We bought him three pairs of jeans six months ago and they're already too short for him."

Casey reached out and affectionately ruffled the curly brown hair so like her own. "Oh, well! Since he'd already started to wear holes in the knees I guess it's no great loss. He can always use them to play in. Come through here, Sharon," Casey invited, motioning toward the side gate which led to the backyard. "It'll be cooler by the pool."

Jonathan, apparently unwilling to accept a change of subject, wriggled in Sharon's arms until she let him down. He ran to catch up with his mother and asked, "Can't I wear them to school, Mom? Brian Fulsom and Freddie Gilmore wear theirs, and they look hecka bad.''

"Hecka what?" Sharon arched her brows quizzically, her eyes twinkling as Jonathan's wide grin displayed the gap where a baby tooth used to be.

"You know, Auntie Sharon," he declared importantly. "Hecka bad!"

"Yes, Auntie Sharon," Casey mimicked teasingly, turning to latch the gate after Sharon stepped through the opening. "Everyone knows what 'hecka bad' means."

Before Sharon had a chance to further disillusion Jonathan with her ignorance, a loud Tarzan yell sounded from the backyard. There was the sound of a splash, and as though galvanized by an electrical charge, Jonathan gave an ear-splitting screech and tore off in the direction of the pool.

Casey winced and muttered disgustedly, "Like father, like son."

Taking advantage of Jonathan's departure, Sharon nudged Casey with her elbow and said, "For heaven's sake, Casey, will you tell me what 'hecka bad' means before my image is permanently ruined?"

Casey laughed and led the way around the side of the house. "It's the 'in' phrase at school."

"I didn't know first graders had an 'in' phrase," Sharon grumbled.

"Don't let Jon hear you," Casey warned. "With only another week of school left, he already considers himself a second grader."

"Uh, oh," Sharon said with a grin. "A slip like that would have gotten me in worse trouble than not knowing what 'hecka bad' means."

Casey took pity on her. "As far as I can figure out it's everything from terrific to fabulous."

"Ahhh," Sharon sighed as her suspicion was confirmed. "When I was Jonathan's age everything was boss."

"You got it!"

Sharon chuckled and shrugged her shoulders in a gesture of resignation. "I no sooner get used to one word, when he springs another one on me. What ever happened to awesome?"

"It's as dead as the dodo bird, which is what I'll be if I don't get that barbecue going."

As the afternoon progressed Sharon was glad she'd accepted Casey and Chad Walker's invitation for dinner. The last few weeks she'd nearly worked herself to a standstill, dropping into bed each night in complete exhaustion. When Casey had phoned her last night at the restaurant, Sharon had been restless, irritated and glad for an excuse to relax.

Yet she could see that the extra hours she'd been putting in at work had served their purpose. She sometimes managed to get through the day without thinking of Rob more than half a dozen times. Of course, when he did pop into her mind his image usually lingered for hours, but she couldn't let herself worry about that. Given time she was certain to get over her fixation, even it if killed her.

As she laughed at Chad and Jonathan's antics in the pool, Sharon shifted restlessly and pressed her hand against her middle. She was uncomfortably full and mentally chastised herself for finishing the juicy hamburger Chad had grilled for her. She hadn't been eating much lately and stuffing herself had caused her stomach to revolt.

"What's the matter, Sharon?"

Casey had returned from putting her daughter to bed, and now glanced pointedly at the hand Sharon was rubbing against her stomach. "Aren't you feeling well?"

"I'm as healthy as a horse, as usual." Hoping to erase the worried look in her friend's eyes, she abruptly changed to a subject that was guaranteed to divert Casey's attention. "Did the baby wake up when you put her in her crib?"

Patricia Kim was a fairly new arrival to the Walker household. At four months of age she had every member of her family, and especially her godmother, Sharon, wrapped around her fat little finger. Jonathan adored his baby sister, which was a relief to his parents. Because Chad had adopted Jonathan, Casey's son from her first marriage, both he and Casey had been afraid Jon might be jealous at having to share his new father with another child.

They needn't have worried, thought Sharon, glancing toward the pool where a tall, fair-haired man was patiently teaching Jon to dive. Chad was careful to give both of his children equal attention. Even before he and Casey had married, in the days when he despaired of ever gaining Casey's love, Chad had lavished his affection on Jon. As a result, the little boy was confident and self-assured, and had long since ceased to ask about the father he had never seen often enough to get to know.

"Sharon, sometimes I swear I could shake you!"

She nearly jumped out of her skin as the sound of Casey's voice, raised in exasperation, broke into her thoughts. "I guess I kind of drifted away for a moment," Sharon replied sheepishly.

"You always go off into your own little world when you want to evade an issue," Casey complained, her mouth firming with determination as she eyed her friend.

With an apologetic grimace Sharon shrugged and managed to avoid Casey's eyes. "I'm sorry to be such a wet blanket, Casey. I've been tired lately."

"If those shadows under your eyes are to be believed, you outdistanced tired a long time ago."

"Don't fuss, little mother," Sharon said with a smile. "Indigestion is a good builder of moral fiber and might keep me from overeating in the future."

Casey plopped down in the bright yellow wicker patio chair opposite Sharon's and watched her friend with frowning concentration. "Marilyn told me you looked like hell when she met you for lunch last week. Have you been to a doctor?"

"He'd just tell me to drink plenty of liquids and stay in bed."

"Speaking of bed," Casey said, undeterred by the impatience in Sharon's voice. "Why are you having trouble sleeping?"

"I've had a lot on my mind, Casey."

The other woman hesitated as though uncertain how to voice her next question. "Have you had second thoughts, Sharon?"

Sharon's mind drew a blank as she glanced at Casey. "I'm not sure I know what you're talking about."

Casey bit her lip and took the time to draw in a deep breath. "Are you worried about your decision to have a baby by artificial insemination?"

Sharon's breath escaped in a tired sigh, and she leaned back in her chair feeling acutely depressed. She had deliberately kept herself from thinking about her plan to become a single parent, but Casey's question forced instant reevaluation.

She thought back to the afternoon she had first talked to Casey about her desire to have a baby. She and Marilyn had returned to Casey's house after Patricia Kim's christening, and Chad had changed his clothes and taken Jonathan to his soccer practice. The three women had been having coffee together in the kitchen when Sharon had dropped her bombshell.

Marilyn's support she'd taken for granted, but Casey's reaction had surprised her. "Have you thought about the problems you're going to have to face, Sharon?"

"I've thought of little else," she admitted. "Raising a child alone won't be easy, but I'll manage."

"Of course you will," Marilyn said encouragingly. "God knows you've had enough practice."

"That's not the point," Casey insisted, tapping her finger against the cup she held between her hands. "I know what it's like to raise a child alone and it can cause a lot of stress."

"I know there'll be difficulties," Sharon responded quietly.

"I'll help you all I can," Marilyn promised, reaching over to pat her sister on the arm.

"Of course you'll help," Casey retorted impatiently, "we'll all help, but that's not what I'm getting at. No matter how much support and encouragement you receive from your friends and family, you'll still be an unwed mother. I know in these enlightened times there's not supposed to be a stigma attached to the term, but there are a great many exceptions to the rule."

"I can stand up to ridicule, Casey."

"I know you can," she replied seriously. "But will you be so strong when your child is slighted by his friends? You know what it was like for Jonathan when the kids thought he didn't have a father. But he at least had a way to retaliate. He *had* a father, even though Hugh never bothered to visit him."

"I don't have another alternative," Sharon said, closing her eyes on a rush of emotion. "Michael and I were cheated of the children we would have had together. I lost him, but I haven't lost the ability to bear a child. I have to do this, Casey."

Remembering her certainty on that day nearly three months ago, Sharon wondered where all her confidence had gone. Since she'd decided not to see Rob again her days had been filled with an apathetic resignation. She no longer looked forward to receiving notification from the sperm bank. She was better off alone, she thought bitterly. The way she'd been feeling lately she needed another problem about as much as she needed a hole in the head.

Her face must have reflected the harshness of her thoughts, and she looked away from the concern in Casey's eyes. She shrugged her shoulders disconsolately. "I kept my appointment with the sperm bank in Oakland, but they have a long waiting list. They're going to notify me as soon as they have an opening."

"And is the waiting getting to you?"

Sharon's mouth firmed with irritation, and she answered before she had time to think. "The waiting's the least of my worries!"

"Then what *is* troubling you, Sharon?"

The question was spoken in a soft voice, but Sharon couldn't ignore the light of battle in her friend's eyes. Trying to con Casey was like trying to leap a tall building in a single bound. Easy for Superman, she thought, but an ordinary mortal was likely to land with a terrific splat. Too mentally tired to manufacture an alibi, Sharon admitted the worst. "I'm exhausted, depressed and absentminded," she recounted angrily, "and if you add bitchy and frustrated to the list you've pinned the tail on the donkey. I swear I had more control of myself when I was twelve."

"Maybe that's your trouble," Casey remarked gently.

Sharon had shifted her attention to the far corner of the yard, which contained the redwood-latticed gazebo that enclosed Chad and Casey's hot tub. But the unaccustomed hesitancy in Casey's voice drew her complete attention. "What is?"

"At twelve you had to be strong because you felt you had to hold your family together after your mother died. Maybe it's time you broke loose and lost a little of that control you mentioned."

A vivid memory of two bodies joined together in total intimacy entered Sharon's mind, and the laugh she uttered was completely without humor. "Oh, I broke loose all right," she muttered darkly. "That's why I'm frustrated and depressed. Being tired is a result of trying to forget my stupidity!"

Casey's eyes widened in surprise as she noticed the embarrassed expression on her friend's face. Sharon usually managed to keep her emotions well hidden, but Casey knew her too well to be fooled by her sarcasm. Something had happened and Casey didn't have to be psychic to know Sharon was having trouble coping with the result. She frowned as she searched for a clue hidden behind Sharon's tense confession. An idea dawned and Casey sat forward with a jerk.

"A man," she whispered, a ripple of excitement adding a sparkle to her eyes.

Sharon hesitated, and then qualified dejectedly. "A sandcastle man."

Five

A what?'' Casey asked faintly, her confusion obvious.

Sharon sighed, almost relieved to have her secret out in the open. "That's the way I think of him," she confessed self-consciously. "I met him a few weeks ago on the beach. He was building a sandcastle."

Casey grinned. "You had me worried there for a minute."

"That's nothing to the way I felt when I first saw him."

"Go on," Casey insisted, the sudden seriousness of her expression encouraging further confidence.

"There's nowhere to go," Sharon lied, nervously gripping the arms of her chair as she returned Casey's stare. "I met him a few times and I haven't seen him since."

"Was that your decision or his?"

Sharon looked down at her feet. "The decision was mine, not that it makes any difference."

With the sensory capability of a true romantic, Casey came to her own conclusion for Sharon's sudden tension. "This guy meant a lot to you, didn't he, Sharon?"

Sharon's flippancy faded in the face of Casey's conviction. "I don't know," she whispered. "I thought of him as a friend until..." Her voice trailed off in perplexity.

"I think you do know, but you're too afraid to admit it."

"Why should I be afraid?" she asked defensively.

"Because of Michael."

As she heard Michael's name on Casey's lips, Sharon resisted the impulse to flinch. "There was nothing wrong with my relationship with Michael. In fact, quite the opposite is true. He taught me how special the relationship between a man and a woman can be."

"I know that," Casey said. "You were the one who made me see how lucky I was to have a future with Chad. When I saw how much courage it took for you to go on without Michael, I felt like a sniveling coward."

Sharon shifted nervously. "Make up your mind, you goose. First you tell me I'm afraid and next you praise me for my courage."

As Casey replied, her usual grin was missing. Instead her face wore a solemn expression, her eyes intent and serious. "Fear doesn't cancel out bravery, Sharon. I finally showed bravery when I faced my fear of marriage and gave my relationship with Chad a chance. In all the years I've known you," she continued after a slight pause, "you've never let any of the men you've dated get close enough to establish a relationship with you."

"I just wasn't interested," Sharon exclaimed defensively.

"That may be true," Casey agreed, "but even if you had been interested you would have been too scared to do anything about it. Isn't that why you stopped seeing your sandcastle man?"

The words were sharp and to the point, and Sharon looked at Casey as though she'd grown two heads. "I chose to remain free of involvement. Is that a crime?"

"It is if you based your decision on fear. Because you lost the man you loved, you've been afraid to let yourself care for anyone else for fear of losing him, too. Either that or you've made Michael's memory into a shrine in your heart, and you can't face the guilt you might feel if you supplanted him with another man."

Casey had hit the nail on the head and this time Sharon couldn't stop herself from physically recoiling from the truth. She felt the blood receding from her face, and her eyes were tortured as she looked at her friend. "Please, Casey," she whispered, biting down on her lower lip until its trembling stopped. "I don't want to talk about this anymore. I just can't!"

Casey paused as though she were carefully considering her words. "You know I'm here if you need me?"

Sharon nodded and forced a smile. "I know you are, Casey."

Casey's answering grin held warmth and affection. "If I let you off the hook, will you promise me something?"

Sharon's affirmative nod was relieved and Casey said, "Will you promise to think about your feelings for the man you met?"

Sharon was impatient with her friend's persistence, but she tried not to show her irritation. She knew that Casey was only trying to help. Sharon nodded and rose to her feet. "I promise, you irrepressible match-maker," she said, bending to pull Casey out of her chair. "Come on, my friend. Get off your duff and walk me to my car."

Sharon couldn't seem to forget the promise she had given Casey, and during the long drive home she had more than enough time to come to terms with the things Casey had said to her. She realized that her friend was right as she drove into the carport beside her apartment building and shut off the engine. She leaned her elbow against the steering wheel and rested her forehead against her palm.

Sharon knew that she was frightened of caring too much for Rob. She wanted to protect herself against the pain she'd suffered when she lost Michael. She tried to visualize Michael's face and the image was disturbingly vague. She'd held herself aloof from Rob because she couldn't stand the thought of putting another man in Michael's place. The decision had been a conscious one and, as she remembered the guilt she'd felt upon awakening in Rob's bed, she sighed, then slowly stepped out of her car.

Sharon's footsteps lagged as she climbed the stairs to the upper landing, her fatigue more mental than physical. As soon as she entered her apartment and slid the deadbolt into place she headed for the bedroom. She flicked on the overhead light as she crossed the threshold and grabbed a nightgown from the bottom drawer of her dresser. The thought of a shower made her hurry into the bathroom with more eagerness than she'd felt all day. Hopefully she would be able to relax her tense muscles beneath the steamy spray. Afterward she might manage to get some sleep and put off thinking about the contradictions in her life until tomorrow.

After her shower Sharon haphazardly dried herself and pulled a cotton nightgown over her head. As she blow-dried her hair she deliberately kept her mind blank, soothed into a somnolent state by the repetition of her movements.

With her hair still slightly damp she automatically tidied up the bathroom before leaving. Over the years she'd become such a creature of habit that she irritated herself, and her mouth quirked wryly as she turned off the bathroom light.

She returned to the bedroom and methodically pulled back the comforter. As she folded it neatly at the foot of the bed she noticed the tension in her hands. She absently smoothed the quilted fabric. It was then she realized she must face the truth about herself if she were to find any peace of mind. The thought was oddly comforting. She'd hidden from herself long enough. Though Sharon didn't want to admit it, Casey had certainly reached the right conclusion. She was an emotional coward who had chosen to exist in a vacuum rather than live life to its fullest.

With a groan she rushed across the room and turned off the light. A pale stream of moonlight guided her as she returned to bed, and she slipped between the cool sheets as though she were seeking a place to hide. She pulled the blankets up to her neck and stared blindly up at the ceiling. A long time passed before she was able to relax enough to fall asleep.

Sharon's slumber that night was disturbed, and when she opened her eyes the next morning she felt exhausted. For a moment she considered phoning Claudia to tell her she wouldn't be in to work, but immediately realized the futility of such a decision. She knew her depression wasn't going to go away and it was time she took herself in hand. There was no place in her life for self-pity or useless regrets. She had chosen weeks ago to sever her relationship with Rob, and if her decision had created a backlash of loneliness she had no one to blame but herself.

With forced enthusiasm she pushed the covers aside and slid out of bed. She was beginning to straighten when she felt her insides churn sickeningly. She rushed into the bathroom and emptied her stomach, convinced she was coming down with some kind of flu bug. She felt better after she brushed her teeth and took a shower, and by the time she had eaten a slice of toast and drunk a glass of milk her mysterious malaise had disappeared.

While she waited for the coffee to brew, Sharon decided to check her calendar. She fought back a sudden reoccurrence of nausea as she frantically counted the days that had elapsed since the night she'd spent with Rob. It couldn't be true, she thought, afraid to believe in something she wanted more than anything else in the world. Just to be sure she double-checked the dates and then stood swaying in shocked realization.

She was never late, she thought, leaning against the doorway as she gazed into space. She had always been predictably regular. Either her system had gone haywire because of emotional stress, or else she...! Sharon pressed a shaking hand against her stomach. It was then she knew, with an instinct she had no reason to question, that the lovemaking she remembered so vividly had produced a child.

She decided to sit down before her legs completely gave way. She pulled a kitchen chair over to the window, her thoughts turning inward as she stared down at the shoreline. "Rob," she whispered, her hands clutching the windowsill. In her mind's eye she saw a man with golden hair, a magical castle at his feet.

Then she realized she'd never truly given Rob up in her heart. She had callously pushed him from her life, yet he had continued to linger on the periphery of her mind. Had she subconsciously thought to punish him for breaking free of his role of friendship, or had she been punishing herself for her disloyalty to Michael's memory?

Sharon bit down hard on her lower lip, tormented by the questions. With a groan she rested her forehead against the cool glass of the window. Every day without him had given her proof of her self-control, yet what good had it done her? Not a single moment had gone by without her missing him. She might have tried to convince herself of her wish for independence, but that hadn't prevented the loneliness she felt from eating at her soul. Only now did she fully realize how important Rob had become to her. But the realization had come too late.

She and Rob had shared a dream out of time, she thought sadly, with no promises given or commitments made. *And whose fault was that, Sharon,* a taunting inner voice reminded her. Rob had wanted more from her than she had been willing to give, and she had run from him. She couldn't go back to him now that she was carrying his child. The woman he had taken to his bed was certainly old enough to protect herself against pregnancy.

Rob had valued her integrity, she thought painfully. Yet during their time together she had lived a lie of omission. She'd talked to him about so many things, but never once had she expressed her wish to have a baby. The subconscious mind could be a powerful motivating factor, and she shivered at the knowledge. She couldn't help wondering if she'd had another reason for succumbing to the desire she had felt for Rob.

Sharon felt sickened by the guilt she experienced at the thought. She wasn't one of the users of this world…she wasn't! But if she told him about the baby wouldn't she feel obligated to give a full confession? She wondered how he would react if he knew she'd just returned from a consultation appointment with a sperm bank on the day they met?

During the short time she'd spent with Rob he had looked at her with admiration and tenderness. She knew she couldn't stand the thought of seeing his beautiful green eyes filled with contempt for her. Again that irritating voice in her head taunted her. *But doesn't he have the right to know he's about to become a father, Sharon?*

Becoming involved with Rob had been a mistake, one she didn't want to compound. She liked her life

the way it was, she told herself staunchly. She didn't
need or want a man to round out her existence, especially someone like Rob. He deserved more from her
than mild affection. It was Michael she loved, would
always love, and it wouldn't be fair to reenter Rob's
life just because she was carrying his child. For all she
knew he might find the idea of becoming a father dis-
tasteful. As a sop to her conscience it was woefully
inadequate, but it was easier to think Rob might feel
trapped by impending fatherhood than to consider the
alternative.

"Enough of this," she muttered fretfully. She was
taking too much for granted. Nibbling her thumb-
nail, a habit she'd outgrown in her teens, Sharon decided to take one step at a time. The first thing she had
to do was have her pregnancy confirmed. Until she
was certain there really was a baby all of this soul-
searching was futile. She couldn't very well plan a future for a child who might not exist!

Her hands lowered to cradle her stomach, and she
closed her eyes and began to pray. "Let it be true," she
whispered. "Dear God in heaven, let it be true."

Sharon never knew how she managed to function
normally during what was left of the morning. She
went about her work in a delirious daze and saw to the
hundred and one details of running a restaurant the
size of Another Touch of Italy. Luckily the cook she'd
trained was doing a superb job in the kitchen. If it had
been left up to her to prepare the meal, she thought in

amusement, the spaghetti would more than likely be glued to the pan. She carried her imaginings one step further, visualizing a supposedly "cooked" lobster rising from the plate and waving its cute little claws at one of the customers.

Sharon was grateful when the lunch rush subsided and Claudia accompanied the last diner to the door. She watched the other woman locking up, suddenly remembering the size of her friend's family. Sharon was impatient to find a good gynecologist, and who better to advise her than Claudia?

"Claudia, can you give me a minute?"

"Sure," she replied with her usual cheerfulness, sidestepping the dining area and approaching the hallway where Sharon stood waiting. "What's up, boss?"

Sharon hesitated before gesturing for the other woman to precede her into her office. While her friend sat on the edge of the desk Sharon began to pace the floor, nervously trying to collect her thoughts. "Claudia, something's happened—I mean I'm almost sure, but of course I'm not completely certain..."

Claudia stared at her normally sane employer, her mouth rounded in surprise. "For heaven's sake, will you quit dithering and tell me what's wrong?"

The alarm in Claudia's voice was unmistakable, and Sharon tried to reassure her with a smile. But as she met the older woman's eyes her grin faltered, changing into a betraying grimace. She could feel a heated flush rise beneath her skin and rushed into speech to cover her embarrassment. "Uhhh, can you recommend a good gynecologist?"

"Of course I..." Sharon's blush, as well as the question, made Claudia stiffen in sudden shock. Her words trailed off into an intense silence as she stared at Sharon. "You don't mean you're...?"

Sharon nodded stiltedly. "I think I'm pregnant, Claudia."

"Oh, no!" Tears burst from beneath Claudia's fluttering lashes, and her face crumpled like a tired child's as she slid from the edge of the desk. Sharon moved forward, appalled at the distress emanating from a woman who held a special place in her life. In a way Claudia was like the mother she had known for such a short time, Sharon realized. Reaching out, she placed her arms around the sadly bowed figure and gave her a hug. "It isn't like that," she murmured gently. "I want this baby very much, Claudia."

Claudia nodded, but refused to meet Sharon's eyes. "I've watched you with my little Carlos, and I know how much love you'd give to a child."

"Then why the long face, my friend?"

Claudia sniffed and raised her eyes. There was dread in the darkness of her gaze. "I'm afraid for you," she whispered.

Sharon frowned, finally realizing the full extent of Claudia's emotional reaction to her announcement. "Why should you be afraid?"

Even as Sharon asked the question a possible answer leaped into her mind, and she sagged with relief. She gripped the other woman's shoulders and gave her a little shake. "I'm perfectly healthy, Claudia. You don't have to worry about me."

"It's not your health I'm worried about—it's your standing in this community."

Sharon drew in a sharp breath. "Why should my position in this community be affected if I choose to have a child?"

Claudia couldn't meet her eyes and stared down at the tips of her shoes. Her gamine face became mottled with color. Suddenly Sharon was reminded of Casey's words on the subject of unwed mothers, and she took pity on the first real friend she'd made after moving here from Pleasanton. "I'm not angry with you for caring enough to be honest with me, Claudia. Please, just tell me the worst."

At the dry inflection in Sharon's voice Claudia chuckled and moved around the desk. She plopped down in Sharon's chair. "Beauty before youth," she muttered incorrigibly.

Sharon was happy to see her friend's usual sense of humor surface. "Be my guest," she said with a gesture of acceptance. "Now, start talking!"

"I've lived in Mill Valley for many years, Sharon. Some of the most influential citizens in this area have chosen to patronize your restaurant. They're good people, but this community is largely comprised of an older generation. Sometimes they judge others more rigidly than they should.''

''And you're afraid that once my condition becomes known the business will suffer?''

Claudia nodded. ''It's a possibility, *niña*.''

''A distinct possibility,'' Sharon repeated slowly. She bunched her hands into fists at her side and yet held her head at a proud angle as she remarked stoically, ''That's just a chance I'm going to have to take!''

Claudia inclined her head in a gesture of acceptance. With the nervous energy that made her such an excellent manager, Claudia slid open the top drawer of the desk and pulled out a notepad and pencil. Never taking her eyes from Claudia's fluttering hands, Sharon moved around the corner of the desk. She shifted anxiously as she glanced over the other woman's shoulder. ''Dr. Lawrence Mason,'' she murmured. ''Was he the one who delivered Carlos?''

''He also delivered Ramón,'' she corrected.

''But Ramón is seventeen,'' she said. ''Are you certain Dr. Mason isn't past his prime?''

Claudia tore the sheet off the pad. Handing it to Sharon, she said, ''If you call now you might be able to get an appointment for tomorrow afternoon.''

''But are you sure he's—''

''Would I recommend someone with one foot in the grave and the other on a banana peel?'' Claudia snapped, folding her arms across her bosom with a spark of indignation in her eyes.

Sharon's glance was apologetic, yet she remained unconvinced. "I'm sorry, Claudia," she said quietly. "I'm just very uptight about this. I want only the best for my baby."

"You are my dear friend," Claudia explained reassuringly, "and I want only the best for you. Dr. Mason is no spring chicken, but he knows the baby business from bonnets to booties. Anyway," she concluded, her lips twitching as she tried to keep a straight face, "if you aren't happy with him I promise to take over cleaning the toilets until you deliver."

Sharon laughed and patted Claudia's shoulder as the other woman got to her feet. "The way my stomach's been acting up you'll probably end up scrubbing them anyway."

"My old bones don't bend that far," Claudia retorted, sticking an impudent tongue out at her employer as she passed. Opening the door, she turned to give Sharon a thumbs up sign before closing it quietly behind her.

Sharon was still smiling as she dialed the number Claudia had given her and was positively euphoric after she had talked with the receptionist. Just knowing she was seeing the doctor the next afternoon was a positive step into the world of the expectant mother. It was a world that she had nearly given up hope of belonging to, she thought, as she replaced the receiver in its cradle.

Yet did she really belong? she worried, pressing a hand against her stomach in a protective gesture. Fear was suddenly a metallic taste in her mouth as she realized she might be wrong about being pregnant. She'd read about false pregnancies, when a woman's body has all the usual symptoms that in the end prove to be psychosomatic. Could this have happened to her? She tried to push the troublesome thought from her mind, but it persisted.

Leaning back in her chair she closed her eyes tiredly. There were too many problems to think about . . . too many troubles to face. She wanted to shut herself away from reality, and she was suddenly transported back to a sandy shoreline where once again she saw a pair of laughing green eyes. For just an instant she choked on the threat of tears before she deliberately banished the memory. She had no time for the past, she thought stringently. Right now the present posed enough difficulties for her to handle.

Six

———

By the time Sharon arrived at the clinic, she was so nervous her pen kept sliding out of her fingers as she filled out the necessary registration forms. Once that task was accomplished she glanced around the waiting room and noticed the soothing powder blue color of the walls. She was not in the least calmed by her surroundings. In fact, she wondered how in the world she was going to pass the time until her name was called. She must have looked as though she were ready to run screaming from the room because the woman seated next to her struck up a conversation. "My name's Carole," she said with a friendly grin. "Are you a patient of Dr. Barnes?"

"Mine's Sharon, and no," she replied, giving the other girl a relieved glance, "my appointment is with Dr. Mason."

Carole, who was quite obviously pregnant and, in Sharon's estimation, couldn't be more than a day over twenty, smiled and nodded. "I understand he's very good."

"He delivered two of my friend's children, and she thinks so," Sharon replied.

"All of the doctors here are great," Carole said enthusiastically. "I chose Dr. Barnes because he delivered my sister's baby a couple of years ago. Sheila and my brother-in-law thought he was terrific." Carole gestured toward the other women scattered around the room. "Are you here for the same reason as the rest of us balloons?"

Sharon flushed self-consciously and nodded her head. "Yes, but I'm new to this," she admitted wryly.

"Don't look so worried," Carole giggled, "it only gets worse. Just wait until you can't sleep because junior's playing basketball in your tummy."

A nurse stepped into the waiting room at that moment and announced, "Carole Davis?"

"Whoops," Carole grinned, struggling to her feet. "Roll call at last, and I do mean roll!"

After they said their goodbyes and the other woman disappeared around the corner, Sharon began to squirm. Without Carole's friendly company to pass the time, she was becoming increasingly aware of the unyielding surface of the chair in which she sat. Its curved bucket shape had looked so comfortable when she had first arrived, yet now she felt as though she were sitting on a rock. She thought about standing, but quickly decided against it. In her current frame of mind she was likely to start pacing. Although she felt like a hysterical idiot, she didn't want to look like one.

"Sharon Vecchio?"

Sharon was so deep in her own thoughts that she was unaware of the woman who suddenly materialized by her side. As a result, when the nurse spoke her name she jumped about a foot and practically yelled, "Yes!"

The woman took immediate interest in a wrinkle on the front of her uniform, which consisted of a pale lemon jacket and matching slacks. Her broad face remained composed, but Sharon was suspicious. She was sure she saw the nurse's lips twitch.

"We've run into a slight problem," the nurse finally murmured.

Sharon's eyes widened in alarm. She immediately tried to remember the questions on the forms she'd filled out. Could they tell she wasn't pregnant by the answers she'd given? As soon as the question entered her mind she knew she was being silly. Of course they couldn't determine pregnancy without performing the proper test. She was becoming paranoid, yet putting a name to her behavior didn't make her feel any better.

Drawing a shaky breath into her lungs she leaned back and tried to loosen her tense fingers from the edge of the chair. When they reluctantly responded to her mental command, the perspiration-soaked palms made a loud sucking sound against the seat. This time the nurse didn't try to hide her amusement, and Sharon flushed in embarrassment.

Moistening her dry lips with the tip of her tongue, Sharon muttered, "A problem?"

Nurse Montgomery, as the name tag pinned above the woman's ample chest proclaimed, smiled and nodded. "Nothing drastic," she said reassuringly, "but we are going to have to change your appointment. Dr. Mason just got a call from the hospital and is off to deliver a baby."

Sharon must have looked shell-shocked because Nurse Montgomery hurriedly added, "Or you could see one of our other staff physicians if you'd rather."

"If I'd rather?" Sharon's voice emerged as a squeak, and she closed her eyes as relief flooded through her. "Oh yes, I'd rather, all right. If I don't get this over with today I'm going to go crackers."

The other woman laughed and motioned for Sharon to follow her. "Do you have a preference?"

"I beg your pardon?"

"Would you rather see Dr. Barnes or Dr. Mitchel?"

Remembering Carole, Sharon blurted, "Dr. Barnes, please."

Nurse Montgomery nodded and began to search through the files on the reception desk. "He'll be a few minutes," she warned, gesturing toward a door on her left. "He's with another patient right now."

Take 4 Books
–and a Mystery Gift–
FREE

**And preview exciting new Silhouette Desire novels
every month—as soon as they're published!**

Silhouette Desire®

Yes...Get 4 Silhouette Desire novels (a $9.00 value) and a Mystery Gift FREE!

SLIP AWAY FOR AWHILE ... Let Silhouette Desire novels draw you into a world of passion, sensuality, desire, seduction, and love fulfilled. You'll share the drama and romance of successful women in charge of their careers and their lives ... women who face the challenges of today's world to make their dreams come true—in a series of novels written for women who want a more sensual, provocative reading experience.

EVERY BOOK AN ORIGINAL ... Every Silhouette Desire novel is a full-length story, never before in print, superbly written to give you more of what you want from romance. Start with 4 new Silhouette Desire novels—a $9.00 gift from us to you—along with a free Mystery Gift, with no obligation to buy another book now or ever.

YOUR FAVORITE AUTHORS ... Let your favorite authors—such as Stephanie James, Diana Palmer, Dixie Browning, Ann Major, Doreen Owens Malek, Janet Joyce, and others—take you to a whole other world.

ROMANCE-FILLED READING ... Each month you'll receive modern love stories that begin where other romances leave off. Silhouette Desire novels take you *beyond* the others and into a world of love fulfilled and passions realized. You'll share precious, private moments and secret dreams ... experience every whispered word of love.

NO OBLIGATION... Each month we'll send you 6 new Silhouette Desire novels as soon as they are published, without obligation. If not delighted, simply return them within 15 days and owe nothing. Or keep them, and pay just $11.70 for all six books. And there's never an additional charge for shipping or handling.

SPECIAL EXTRAS FOR HOME SUBSCRIBERS ONLY... When you take advantage of this offer and become a home subscriber, we'll also send you the Silhouette Books Newsletter FREE with each book shipment. Every informative issue features news about upcoming titles, interviews with your favorite authors, even their favorite recipes.

So send in the postage-paid card today, and take your fantasies further than they've ever been. The trip will do you good!

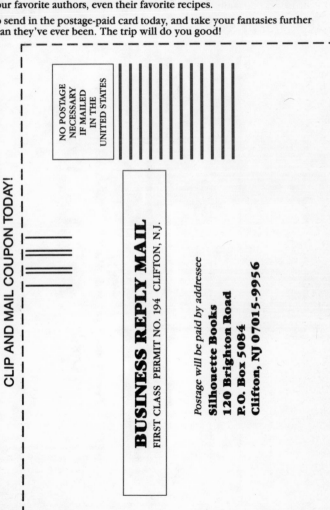

CLIP AND MAIL COUPON TODAY!

NO POSTAGE
NECESSARY
IF MAILED
IN THE
UNITED STATES

BUSINESS REPLY MAIL

FIRST CLASS   PERMIT NO. 194   CLIFTON, N.J.

Postage will be paid by addressee

Silhouette Books
120 Brighton Road
P.O. Box 5084
Clifton, NJ 07015-9956

Take your fantasies further than they've ever been. Get 4 Silhouette Desire novels (a $9.00 value) plus a Mystery Gift FREE!

Then preview future novels for 15 days—
FREE and without obligation. Details inside.

Your happy endings begin right here.

Silhouette Desire ®

Silhouette Books, 120 Brighton Rd., P.O. Box 5084, Clifton, NJ 07015-9956

☐ Yes, please send me FREE and without obligation, 4 brand new Silhouette Desire novels along with my free Mystery Gift. Unless you hear from me after I receive my 4 FREE books, please send me 6 new Silhouette Desire novels to preview each month as soon as they are published.

I understand that you will bill me a total of just $11.70, with no additional charges of any kind. **There is no minimum number of books that I must buy, and I can cancel at any time. The first 4 books and Mystery Gift are mine to keep.**

NAME _____
(please print)

ADDRESS _____

CITY _____ STATE _____ ZIP _____

SILHOUETTE DESIRE is a registered trademark.

Prices and terms subject to change.
Your enrollment is subject to acceptance by Silhouette Books.

CTDN25

As the nurse spoke she withdrew a tan folder from the orderly stack and took a few moments to glance at the contents. Sharon noticed her name was neatly typed on the right-hand corner of the file. Somehow, seeing her chart brought about a renewal of confidence. Sharon smiled brightly and said, "I don't mind waiting."

When she stated her willingness to wait, the pleasant-faced nurse reached for a pen. "I have a few questions to ask," she explained as she began to write, "and then we can get down to business."

Her few questions took a full five minutes, and Sharon was at the point of biting her nails all the way down to the first knuckle. She was saved by the calming influence of Mrs. Montgomery, who joked with her in an effort to relieve her obvious tension. Finally the other woman closed the chart with a snap and grinned at Sharon over the top. "Now that the dirty work is over we can move along to the irritating part."

The nurse bent down and when she straightened she had a plastic container in her hand. She wrote Sharon's name on a piece of tape and stuck it on the side of the cup. "The bathroom's the third door on your right. Just leave the specimen on the ledge and return here."

Sharon followed instructions with the enthusiasm of a zombie. She'd run through such a gamut of emotions during the last hour that she was now numb. When she was eventually led into an examining room and told to disrobe, she wondered if she would ever feel normal again. She had shifted from nervous to scared, and then to just plain petrified.

Her mouth twisted into a parody of a smile as she stepped into a curtained alcove and put on a shapeless white gown with an open back. Sharon was surprised when she was able to move her feet and completely stupefied when she actually managed to climb onto the examining table. Her heart pounded so heavily she was certain the walls must be reverberating with the sound.

Perched on the paper-covered table, Sharon tried to look nonchalant in case the nurse returned. The friendly woman already had reason to believe that her patient was a basket case; she didn't need further convincing. Yet it was darned difficult to maintain a semblance of dignity under the circumstances, Sharon thought, attempting to smooth out an uncomfortable wrinkle in the paper.

She only made matters worse and what was once a tiny ridge soon felt like a fissure the size of the San Andreas Fault. She might have been able to solve the problem if her hands had been free, but one was busy keeping her back end protected from drafts, while the other was trying to prevent the crumpled sheet covering her lap from sliding onto the floor.

Sharon nibbled the inside of her upper lip and pondered her problem. With growing frustration she realized that she couldn't call for help. By now she was shaking so badly her teeth were chattering and her heart was pounding like an out-of-control locomotive. She was thinking that her nerves couldn't stand much more stress when two sharp raps warned her of the doctor's arrival.

It was then that she understood the expression scared stiff. She didn't know whether to throw up or pass out, so she did neither. Instead her spine stiffened and her back assumed a posture that her German grandmother would have commended.

A moment later a tall man entered the room, his head bent as he studied her chart. Sharon stared at the man and felt laughter bubble up in her throat. Things like this just *couldn't* happen in real life, she thought.

When her mouth opened and a giggle emerged, she blinked in confusion. She couldn't believe the sound had come from her traitorous throat. Laughter was the farthest thing from her mind. There was nothing ... absolutely nothing ... amusing to be found in her present situation. Silently she prayed she was having a nightmare. Miracles did happen, she told herself wildly. With any luck she would soon wake up in her own bed.

Just then the doctor looked up. As recognition sparked in a pair of eyes as green as a forest glade, Sharon barely managed to stop herself from throwing the sheet over her head. He'd already seen her, she decided with depressing logic. Hiding now wouldn't work. Instead she tilted her chin and met his eyes with as much courage as she could muster. She saw his features register shock, disbelief and finally complete and total realization. When his glance lowered to a small slip of paper clipped to her chart she heard him mutter, "Dear God!"

Sharon cleared her throat and smiled sickly. "He's too late to help me out of this one!"

Rob's head jerked and his eyes narrowed as he studied her. "You've got that right, honey!"

When another knock sounded on the door and Rob turned aside to open it, her relief was so profound she nearly slipped off of the examining table. While he spoke in whispered accents to his extremely puzzled nurse, Sharon stared at an individual as far removed from her sandcastle man as it was possible to be. His blond hair was meticulously combed, the thick strands no longer tumbling boyishly onto his forehead. The tanned legs she had thought so sexy were covered by well-pressed black slacks, and a pale blue dress shirt was visible beneath the opening of a white laboratory jacket. When Dr. Robert Barnes closed the door on his departing nurse with a decisive slam, Sharon knew her reprieve was over. With the swiftness of an unrepentant coward she lowered her lashes to shield her expression.

Yet she could feel his eyes on her, and she began to fidget uneasily as she stared at a shiny aluminum wastepaper basket in the corner. She could feel her cheeks flushing and it seemed to her that Rob was getting a perverse pleasure from her embarrassment. Just for an instant she sneaked a glance at his face and then wished she hadn't.

His expression no longer registered stunned disbelief, and she was unable to look away from him. Instead she saw a combination of anger and pain tighten his features into an accusatory mask. "I thought we should have privacy for this particular—" he hesitated, as his mouth twisted into sarcastic lines "—examination."

"If you'll just let me explain."

"Explain why I woke up one fine morning to find you gone?" He laughed harshly, his face tinged by a dark tide of color. "You turned one of the most beautiful experiences of my life into a damned one-night stand, Sharon. I almost went crazy trying to find you, do you know that?"

She saw the extent of the hurt in his eyes. "Rob, I'm so sorry," she said.

"I practically haunted the beach for three damn weeks. I didn't know your last name, let alone where you lived. All I could do was wait and hope you'd come back. When you didn't return I couldn't stand the sight of my beach house. I decided to stay on my houseboat in Sausalito where I wasn't reminded of you constantly."

Sharon's eyes were full of misery. "I never meant to cause you so much trouble, Rob. I didn't think—"

"That's right," he interrupted frigidly, "you didn't think, Sharon. But believe me, I've had plenty of opportunity for soul-searching. When I realized how cleverly you covered your tracks I decided you must have lied to me."

For a moment her entire reasoning ability froze, then speeded up with a vengeance. He'd found out about her appointment with the sperm bank; he must have! As soon as the illogical thought formed she called herself every kind of a fool. There was no way he could have discovered her secret, she realized, drawing a relieved breath. Guilt was making her crazy!

Her voice was weak when she finally pulled herself together enough to respond, "Lied to you?"

A muscle in his jaw pulsed visibly. "Didn't you?" he asked bitterly. "Tell me, did your husband question your absence that night, or was he away on a business trip when you decided to take a lover?"

Sharon paled, appalled at the conclusion he had drawn from her disappearance. "I have no husband!"

"Then whoever it is you're involved with," he muttered impatiently. "What other reason would you have for running out on me, Sharon?"

"You don't understand," she cried, wincing at the suspicion in his voice. "Everything happened so fast. Is it any wonder I couldn't cope with our relationship?"

She paused, searching his eyes for understanding. Instead she encountered a coldness in his unfaltering gaze that made her ache with regret. She knew Rob deserved an explanation for her cowardice, and she attempted to make him understand the confusion and shame she'd felt after their lovemaking. As he listened, some of the hardness disappeared from his face. By the time her faltering words subsided into a tense silence his expression was one of sadness.

"You could have discussed your feelings with me," he accused. "You didn't have to run away."

She shrugged her shoulders and tried to stop the trembling of her mouth. "What was I going to say?"

"Something—anything," he retorted.

Her laugh was brittle as she remembered the thoughts that had motivated her flight that morning. "Can't you understand how disgusted I was with myself, Rob? You made me experience emotions I never even knew existed. When I thought about Michael I felt like a traitor to his memory. I had given more of myself to a man I didn't really know than to a man I loved."

He paled and his features lost all expression. "I . . . see!"

"Don't look at me like that," she cried. "It was better for me to leave you without senseless arguments."

He laughed cynically. "Better for you?"

"Better for both of us," she said with gentle dignity. "You deserve more than a woman without a heart to give you, Rob."

"So I was left with nothing," he exclaimed, his eyes flashing bitterly. "All that remained was your sweet scent on my pillows and the memory of your body in my arms. You had no right to make a decision like that on your own, not when it affected my life as well as yours."

"I didn't trust myself to be strong enough to resist your persuasion," she said, only then fully acknowledging the truth of that statement. "I would have looked at you and seen the memory of what we had done together in your eyes. That would have given you an unfair advantage over me, Rob."

"We made love," he interrupted hoarsely. "You had no reason to feel ashamed."

Her smile was sad. "Didn't I?"

Her question made him wince. "No, damn it, you didn't!"

"I did what I thought was right at the time."

"Leaving me without a word of explanation was not only wrong—it was cruel, Sharon."

She knew he had a right to be angry with her, but she didn't back down from the decision she had made on that momentous day six weeks earlier. "You knew from the beginning that I wasn't looking for an involvement," she reminded him. "Sharing your bed didn't change the way I felt. As soon as I realized that, I left with as little fuss as possible."

"Then why did you spend the night with me?" he asked angrily. "Was I just a test case, a way for you to find out if you were still alive?"

She gasped and stared at the stranger he'd become. "I don't have to answer that."

"I'll answer for you," he said, his voice deceptively low. "You were more alive in my arms than you've ever been and you enjoyed every minute of it. You twisted and moaned under my body like a wild, wanton creature too long denied the pleasures of the flesh.''

Sharon squeezed her eyes closed and childishly covered her ears with her hands. "I don't want to listen to you!"

"Oh, hell!"

She heard his footsteps approach, but before she could jerk away he captured her wrists between his strong fingers. Ruthlessly her hands were pressed into her lap and held there. She kept her eyes resolutely shut, and yet she didn't have to see him to remember every inch of his powerful frame. Her memory was aided by his clean, male fragrance. She drank in his scent with shuddering pleasure and felt her body's response with resignation.

"Sharon, please look at me," he murmured, his tone distracted.

Warily she lifted her lashes, seduced by the gentleness of his voice. "Don't hate me, Rob."

Her plaintive whisper made him draw in a harsh breath. "I could never hate you, Princess. You can't help not loving me, anymore than I can help the way I feel about you."

"I do care for you, Rob."

"That's enough for now," he said, tracing the shape of her mouth with his gaze. "I expected too much from you too quickly. If I was hurt it was my own damn fault for pressuring you into a relationship you weren't ready for."

"I swear I never meant to hurt you," she exclaimed, her voice cracking with emotion.

"So where do we go from here?"

She stiffened, certain the whole argument was going to resume. "Please, I don't want to go over the whole thing again."

"But we haven't discussed the future," he said in a carefully moderated tone. "I'm afraid you're going to have to listen to me . . . especially now."

He released her wrists and took a single step backward. She studied his tightly controlled features and realized his recent anger had dissipated as though it had never existed. Resentment flashed through her when she compared his poised figure to her current state of disarray. She felt completely drained.

Some of her resentment carried over in her voice when she said, "The way things stand I don't have much choice, do I?"

Her sweeping hand indicated her state of undress. She was surprised, and a little disgruntled, to see his brief smile. "You are in a bit of a quandary at the moment."

Still dazzled by her reaction to his smile, she asked absently, "You spoke of the future?"

His hands moved on the periphery of her vision, and then her heart began to thud when they settled against her neck. "I have the result of your urinalysis."

She nodded unsteadily as her hand began to nervously twist the edge of the sheet covering her legs. "And?"

He misinterpreted the fear he saw in her eyes, and his mouth compressed briefly before he started to speak. "I'm sorry, Sharon."

Tears of disappointment flooded her eyes, and her body swayed toward him. Her mouth was muffled by his jacket as she asked dully, "I'm not pregnant?"

The muscles in his arms contracted in surprise as he pulled her closer. "I'm sorry I didn't take the proper precautions that night, but I didn't expect what happened between us."

From somewhere deep inside she managed to cling to what self-control she still possessed. "It doesn't matter," she responded unemotionally, when what she really wanted to do was sob out her disappointment against his chest.

"Of course it matters," he nearly shouted, drawing back to look into her face with incredulous eyes. "A positive chemical analysis has a very definite outcome. In a matter of months you'll be a mother. And I," he said gently, one hand reaching out to lift her chin until their eyes were level, "will be a father."

She stared at him, only then realizing the significance of his apology. Rob was blaming himself for failing to guard her against pregnancy! She wanted to laugh, she wanted to cry, but above all she wanted to alleviate his guilt. But to do that she would have to tell him she'd wanted to have a child all along, and she could imagine his reaction. He would feel he had been used as a means to an end, and she couldn't stand the thought of seeing a return of his earlier anger. She didn't want to spoil this moment, her first as a prospective mother.

Sharon forgot about the sheet, which slipped unimpeded to the floor. She clutched at Rob's lapels with all the strength her two hands could muster, her eyes glistening with unashamed joy. "I'm really pregnant?"

Rob saw the raw emotion in her eyes and heard the hopeful catch in her breath as she stammered the question. Suddenly there was a new expression on his face, one of shocked understanding. "You want this baby?"

She stared at him, realizing now was the perfect opportunity to tell him about her visit to the sperm bank. No, she wasn't ready to make a full confession—not yet. Instead her eyes drifted closed and she said softly, "Yes, I want this baby very much."

Suddenly Sharon straightened and when her eyes opened there was dread swirling in their dark brown depths. "You're sure?" she demanded, her hands twisting permanent wrinkles into his jacket. "There really is a baby? You haven't made a mistake?"

A wide grin formed on his mouth and he nodded his reassurance. "There really is a baby."

Still unable to accept his judgment she frowned worriedly. "But I haven't actually been examined."

"The lab test is ninety-nine percent conclusive," he said, "but I'll be happy to oblige."

As he spoke he slid his hands across her shoulders, and the gleam in his eyes as he stroked her naked back lacked professionalism. Sharon caught her breath, suddenly remembering that this man who was causing such delicious sensations to course down her spine wasn't her sandcastle man . . . he was her doctor!

With an embarrassed grimace she grabbed at his arms. "You needn't bother, I . . . I'll wait until I can see Dr. Mason. My appointment was really with him, and I wouldn't want to hurt his feelings. After all, we can't—"

Sharon looked everywhere but at Rob as she tried to talk herself out of her predicament. She only became aware of his silent laughter when his arms began to shake. Instantly her self-consciousness was replaced with indignation. "Just what's so funny?"

"You are," he grinned. "Did you really think I was going to complete your examination?"

Her relief was palpable as she said, "I would have died!"

"I'll have you know I'm an excellent doctor," he stated with mock indignation. "But it isn't good practice for a doctor to treat a family member."

Before she had a chance to think Sharon blurted, "We're not related."

With studied deliberation Rob's head lowered as he glanced pointedly at her stomach. Then his eyes slowly traveled upward, lingering longer than necessary at her breasts before finally returning to scrutinize her reddening features. "Aren't we?"

"Well, yes, but I don't . . . I mean you don't have to feel obligated," she stuttered, inwardly cursing herself for the nervousness tying her tongue into knots. "What happened between us was—"

"Beautiful?"

Sharon tried to swallow and failed. How could she deny the beauty of what they had shared? It had been the perfection of their lovemaking that had made her feel so unfaithful to Michael's memory. "Yes, beautiful, but . . ."

His eyes narrowed consideringly as he took note of her growing consternation. "Is there something else you were intending to say?"

"I just want you to know I accept full responsibility for this situation," she said, rushing to get the words out coherently. "You naturally thought a woman my age would be well versed in birth control, but I . . ."

Her voice trickled into guilty silence. Oh, Sharon, she thought in disgust. You should tell him why birth control never entered your mind. He deserves the complete truth. She opened her mouth but no words emerged. She snapped it shut again with exasperation at her continued duplicity.

He waited politely for her to continue. When it became apparent she had said all she was going to say, an unholy gleam lighted his eyes. "But you slipped up?"

She moistened her lips. "Something like that."

Such an understatement couldn't be bettered, but she placed the blame solely on his head. His friendly teasing was rapidly undermining her good sense. This was the man she'd known, she thought, a weaver of dreams who made her feel like a princess. She met his eyes and couldn't resist responding to the warmth she saw in them. The sterile environment of the examining room dissolved and was replaced with a flickering fire in her mind. Friend . . . lover, she wondered disorientedly. Just what was he to her?

She saw his mouth form her name and recognized the hungry urgency of his mesmerizing gaze. As though in a trance she waited while his face drew closer to her own, and she swallowed with difficulty. "Not here," she whispered stiltedly.

"Then where?" he asked hoarsely. "Where, Princess?"

Seven

"If you hadn't seen me today, would you have tried to find me to let me know about the baby, Sharon?"

They were seated together in a dim, air-conditioned restaurant around the corner from the clinic. When Rob asked his question Sharon avoided looking at him. The gray-tinted glass of their secluded alcove gave them an illusion of privacy in the crowded room and also formed a perfect mirror for her strained features.

During dinner they had conversed politely, as though they were on a first date with nothing more on their minds than getting to know each other. Sharon had told him about her restaurant, while Rob related some of the lighter aspects of his profession. She discovered he was an only child who had grown up in Pennsylvania and that his mother and stepfather were living in a retirement community in Florida.

He'd watched her face with intense concentration when she'd described her own family. As she relaxed and became lost in reminiscence she was only vaguely aware of the table being cleared. A waiter had refilled their coffee cups and quickly left them alone, but the interruption abruptly ended her inconsequential chatter. The silence between them lingered and the tension began to mount.

Sharon had imagined herself prepared for a serious shift in their conversation, but when the moment came she felt overwhelmed by a sense of panic. She caught a glimpse of her eyes in the smoked glass. They were wide and frightened, and her mouth looked oddly vulnerable as she parted her lips to form an answer to Rob's question. She haltingly gave him a negative reply, glancing away from her own guilty reflection in time to see the quick flash of anger in his eyes.

"Didn't you think I had a right to know?"

"I never thought in terms of right and wrong," she admitted. "My decision was based on the only facts I had at my disposal. One, we'd made no promises to each other. Two, there was no real commitment between us." Sensing an argument from Rob on the second point, Sharon anticipated his outburst. "All right," she qualified hurriedly, "in my mind there was no commitment between us. You'd been out of my life for several weeks, long before I suspected I might be pregnant. I couldn't just knock on your door and say, 'Hello, I have a surprise for you.' I didn't think you'd be exactly overjoyed at learning you'd fathered a child. You certainly hadn't planned to become a parent.'' No, she thought guiltily, she had been the one with all the plans!

''Is that why you want to assume full responsibility for the baby?'' he asked as he reached across the table for her hand. ''Because you blame yourself for its conception?''

She looked at their entwined fingers and tried to swallow the sudden lump in her throat. Of course she blamed herself, she thought, appalled by the extent of her dilemma. She was pregnant with the child she'd decided to have before she'd even met Rob, although she was too much of a coward to admit the truth to him. *He doesn't ever have to know,* an inner voice tempted insidiously. *He would only be hurt by the knowledge, and you've already caused him enough pain.*

Sharon glanced up at him and saw his eyes cloud with emotion. ''It takes two, honey,'' he said.

''I don't blame you for the baby's conception,'' she whispered. ''I've already told you how much I want this child.''

Rob hesitated, and when he spoke his words held unmistakable conviction. ''So do I, Sharon!''

She almost choked on an indrawn breath, and her eyes looked at him with trepidation. ''You do?''

''Yes.''

Rob released her hand and rose to his feet. He reached inside his sport coat, and when he withdrew his wallet, she watched the movement of his hands in mindless fascination. His motions were assured as he paid for their meal and left a sizable tip; his manner calm. Then he drew her up to stand beside him and bent his head to press a gentle kiss against her mouth. "I want our baby almost as much as I want you, Princess."

Sharon was speechless as she allowed Rob to guide her from the restaurant, and she still hadn't spoken when they reached his car. Her thoughts were a confused jumble and as they drove out of the parking lot she felt as though this day had lasted for a thousand years. When she finally collected herself enough to notice they were headed away from Mill Valley, it was too late for her to protest. Still, she had to say something!

"It's getting late," she remarked in a tight voice. "I really should be starting for home, Rob. Tomorrow is one of our busiest days at the restaurant and I'll have to be there to supervise both lunch and dinner."

Another fabrication to compound her already guilty conscience, she realized as they arrived at the Yacht Club Marina in Sausalito. She sounded so convincing she would soon begin to believe herself. The sun was just going down as Rob helped her from the car, and she shivered when the wind caught her dress.

"The evening's young," he said. "I'll drop you by your car in a little while, but right now I'd like to continue our conversation in comfort."

He soothed her nervousness with a smile and a nod in the direction of the houseboat moored a few feet away. "What do you think of it?"

She looked up at the huge boxlike structure painted a pristine white with red trim. It looks like a giant candy cane, she thought, inwardly cautioning herself against verbalizing such a childish reaction. Instead she glanced at the man walking by her side, "It's very nice." She heard the inane sound of her reply through a roaring in her ears.

He guided her up the dock, and before she knew it she was standing in his living room. She stared at her surroundings, her mouth parted in surprise. The room was large and furnished with a tasteful elegance that took her breath away. Two walls, as well as the entrance, were comprised almost entirely of glass. No matter which way she turned she had a view of sparkling blue-green water, or of neighboring boats in varying sizes and shapes. She turned toward Rob, who was standing in the doorway and obviously waiting for her reaction.

He smiled when he noticed the pleasure in her eyes. "You like?"

"I like very much," she breathed faintly.

"Sit down while I fix us a couple of gin and tonics."

He walked toward a bar that separated the living room from the kitchen area, and Sharon sank down on a plush cream-and-rust divan with a relieved sigh. She was so tense her legs were trembling, and as she watched Rob return with their drinks, she knew her nervousness would increase.

Her deduction proved annoyingly correct when he sat beside her, so close that his muscular thigh brushed her own. She jumped as though touched by a jolt of electricity and felt foolish when she noticed his mouth curve with amusement. She accepted the frosted glass he held out to her and lowered her head to take a sip of the contents. The thick carpet at her feet held her attention as she calculated how soon she could make her escape.

"Do you like the color?"

Her head lifted jerkily and some of the contents of her glass landed on her lap. "What?"

He gestured toward the floor and bent forward to relieve her of her unwanted drink. He placed her glass and his own on a marble-topped end table and then turned to give her a look of inquiry. "You seemed to be admiring the color of my carpet."

"Oh, yes," she muttered distractedly. "It's very... uhhh... pretty."

"And you approve my choice of decor?"

She cleared her throat and stopped twisting the hem of her skirt when she noticed him looking at her hands. "It's lovely."

What a master she was at description, she thought in disgust. Next she would be telling him the wide-screen television in the corner was cute, or the gold-toned appliances in the kitchen were darling. She only hoped he didn't get around to asking her opinion of the Tiffany lamp hanging from the ceiling. Sparkling prisms were reflected through multicolored segments of leaded glass, the escaping light softening to a warm glow. The effect was sensuous, but that particular comparison was best kept to herself!

"Would you like to see the bedroom?"

"No!" Sharon heard the loudness of her voice and closed her eyes to shut out the sight of his wickedly taunting expression. She was acting like an idiot, but she couldn't help herself. The whole of her left side tingled from its close contact with his body, setting off a chain reaction throughout her that dismayed her with its strength.

Gathering what remained of her sanity, she said, "I really should be on my way. I have a long drive ahead of me."

He shifted toward her and braced one arm along the back of the divan. "I thought you said your restaurant was in Mill Valley?"

"Yes, but I live at Stinson Beach."

"You what?" His brow furrowed into a scowl. "You mean you intend to drive all the way to Stinson tonight?"

She tried to smile and failed miserably. With a small shrug of her shoulders she said dryly, "I hadn't actually planned to return this late. You might say I was . . . detained."

He didn't respond to her teasing. If anything, she thought, his features had taken on an even sterner cast, one that went far beyond disapproval. She shifted edgily, glancing at him out of the corner of her eyes. "Is something wrong?"

"Is something wrong?" he exploded, his heated gaze incredulous. "You live at Stinson Beach and work in Mill Valley and you want to know what's bothering me? Haven't you got sense enough not to risk your life on a twisting mountain road, woman?"

She glared at him. "I know that road like the back of my hand."

"When it's shrouded in fog," he yelled, "all you'll be able to *see* is the back of your hand!"

"Don't shout at me," she hollered just as loudly. "I love living by the ocean."

They were at a stalemate, each staring at the other, their faces flushed with temper. Sharon couldn't believe the man before her was the same smiling, gentle, considerate man she had met on the very beach he now seemed to be criticizing. No wonder he hadn't found time to renovate his little cottage, she thought furiously. He probably only used it as a convenient love nest.

She put the thought into words and watched Rob's eyes narrow. "Just what—" he whispered with deceptive softness "—are you implying?"

Sharon swallowed and wondered how this situation had gotten out of hand. They'd been sitting quietly one minute and then in the next were practically tearing each other's hair out. Although she thought that Rob was being unreasonable, she knew that she wasn't exactly an example of cool serenity herself. She couldn't understand why she'd taken such a perverse delight in goading him, especially when she knew he was only concerned for her safety.

She almost never lost her temper, and yet here she was screaming at him like a shrew. She was so out of control she was actually visualizing Rob as an enemy. The thought was sobering. When she suddenly realized the reason for her reaction, she was ill-equipped to handle the truth. With a mumbled excuse she got up and walked over to the window and ran a shaking hand over her tumbled hair.

She felt rather than heard Rob's approach, every nerve in her body alert as he halted behind her. She turned to face him, her eyes shadowed with unhappiness. "I'm not used to being accountable to someone else for my actions," she said in an awkward attempt at apology. "I know you're only thinking of my welfare."

She saw his gaze drop to her mouth, and a pulse throbbed in his cheek as though his teeth were clenched. "I didn't mean to act like an egocentric idiot, Sharon. Being worried about you is no excuse for the way I reacted. You're perfectly capable of making your own decisions."

Sharon was oddly touched by the grudging way he expressed himself. "Even when I don't have the sense to know when to come in out of the fog?"

"So, okay, we're both idiots," he chuckled, and bent to place a smacking kiss against her mouth. "Since we're quite obviously made for each other, let's get married."

The smile that had begun to soften her mouth slipped into a frown at his offhand proposal. "How can you make such an assumption when you don't really know me, Rob?"

Her protest was a clear indication of the doubt she was feeling, but his gaze never faltered as his long, blunt fingers gripped her shoulders. In an odd way his touch was reassuring, the strength of his hands lending emphasis to his words. "I know all that I need to, Sharon. I know you're gentle, sweet and so lovely I ache just looking at you."

Do you also know I'm deceitful? she wondered bitterly. His description of her was spoken with tenderness, the expression on his face was open and trusting. She felt so awful she wanted to crawl in a hole and die. She knew that she didn't deserve his praise or his respect, and her heart ached.

"You're all I want in a woman," Rob continued with complete conviction, "all I'll ever want. The first time I saw you, you looked at me with those big dark eyes of yours and I knew we belonged together."

"But we don't!" As she spoke she wondered who she was trying to convince, herself or Rob. In a desperate attempt at self-assurance she said, "I've lived alone too long. I'd make a lousy wife."

"You'd make a wonderful wife," he countered softly.

Sharon's gaze faltered and her uneasiness increased. All her life she'd hidden her feelings behind a cloak of reserve, carefully guarding herself against impulsive decisions. She had subdued her fiery Italian heritage, well aware of the heartbreak her sister Marilyn's impetuousness often caused her. Instead she had modeled herself after her mother, who had remained calm and unruffled in a household where hot tempers were more often the rule than the exception.

As a result she was accustomed to making decisions only after cautious deliberation. From the moment she'd met Rob, her impulsiveness had been one of the main reasons for her confusion regarding their relationship. Yet before her stood a man who was willing to enter into a marriage based on emotion rather than logic. He knew she didn't love him, but still seemed to think a marriage between them would work. He was asking her to suppress her innate prudence and trust in his feelings for her; to trust that some day she would return his affection and they would live happily ever after. She felt more unsettled than ever. "How can you be so sure, Rob?"

"How can I not when the emptiness I've carried inside for so long was filled by your smile? I'm not a young, insecure boy, Sharon," he remarked firmly. "I know what I want. If my feelings for you were in the least ambiguous, don't you think I would have discovered it before now? When you disappeared I nearly went nuts, especially when I realized I might never see you again.''

She shook her head impatiently. "I'm not doubting you," she said. "It's just difficult for me to believe this is happening. We've known each other such a short time, and I can't help thinking you're mistaken about the way you feel."

"There's not a doubt in my mind," he said with confidence. "I love you, Sharon. I want to be married to you."

She closed her eyes, completely shattered by his admission. Her mouth was dry and her throat hurt when she tried to swallow. With the clumsy precision of a windup doll she turned her back to him and stared blindly into the evening shadows. How long had it been since she had heard those words? she wondered. How long since she had felt secure in a man's love for her?

Once she had viewed marriage as the culmination of everything she had ever hoped her future would hold. Those days had passed like sweet honey, but they had left a bitter residue. She had built her life apart from dreams, apart from love. She could trust herself to control her destiny, and yet loving meant placing her happiness in hands other than her own. There was no security in love—only a vulnerability she never again wanted to experience.

Rob moved to her side. "What do you feel for me, Sharon?"

What did she feel for him? she asked herself, her emotional stability verging on hysteria. She felt wild elation, heat and fire, and singing in her heart. She felt all the things she didn't want to feel, and she was afraid. She didn't want to put a name to what she experienced whenever he was near. To do so would be to tempt a fate that was often a cruel predator, which tore apart dreams and left the dreamer alone and dying. Her eyes were shadowed when she looked at him and whispered, "I don't know."

Rob's lashes lowered briefly. When they lifted there was a deep flaring of sensuality in his eyes. "I think you do know, Sharon."

With a sensation of helplessness she felt her body respond to the desire in his gaze. She was being made love to, and yet there was no physical contact between them. Rob's body was tense, held as stiffly as her own. But there was a knowledge in his eyes that filtered through the silence between them . . . a knowledge of her unwilling attraction to him.

"All right," she said haltingly. "I care for you, Rob. I care for you as a friend."

"We've been friends and lovers," he said, reaching out to brush her cheek with his fingers. "That's a good basis for marriage, Sharon."

She flinched away from his touch. "I don't want to marry you, or anyone else."

"Aren't you forgetting one of the reasons we're having this conversation?" His expression was somber as he lowered his gaze to her stomach. "You're carrying something that in part belongs to me. I want our child to carry my name."

Sharon nodded and attempted to pacify him. "Your name will be on the birth certificate, if that's what you want."

"What I want is for my child to be legitimate."

"In this day and age—" She was cut off before she could complete her sentence, completely dismayed by the look of scorn on his face.

"Oh, no," he exclaimed harshly. "Don't lecture me on how well modern society treats an illegitimate child, Sharon. I've been there, and no way is any child of mine going to suffer the way I did."

Her gaze was filled with consternation and something closely approaching tenderness. "I'm sorry," she said quietly. "I didn't realize. I thought you said your mother and father were living in Florida."

"My mother and stepfather are living there," he explained. "My mother raised me on her own. I was twenty when she finally married."

Sharon hesitated before asking, "And your father?"

"Don't get the wrong idea, Sharon. My father loved my mother and me and spent as much time with us as he could. But he was already committed to a woman who refused to free him from their marriage." He laughed, and the sound was filled with irony. "Divorce wasn't as easy to come by in those days."

"It must have been very difficult for both you and your mother."

Rob nodded. "I grew up in a small town in Pennsylvania that was founded by my father's ancestors. It would have been easier on my mother if we'd moved away, but she wouldn't leave him." He paused, and his eyes held a faraway expression. "He set up a trust fund for my education when I was small. I was fifteen when he died, and I've always been sorry he didn't live long enough to know I'd followed in his footsteps."

"He was a doctor?"

"One of the best," Rob replied. "He was a good man who placed a great deal of trust in human nature until he saw how my mother and I were treated by the upstanding citizens in our community. Everytime he saw me sporting bruises or a black eye he died a little, Sharon. He felt responsible for our suffering, and he knew that deep inside I blamed him, too."

Sharon's heart contracted with pity. "That was a normal reaction for a child, Rob. I'm certain your father understood."

"Maybe he did, Sharon, but I'm the one who bears the scars for the way I sometimes treated him," he said shortly. "I'm the one who stood beside his grave and finally told him how much I loved him, but the admission came too late for both of us."

Sharon's voice was husky with emotion as she murmured, "Oh, Rob!"

His features hardened as he approached her with a prowling stride and reached out to clasp her shoulders. "It's not too late for our baby, Sharon," he said with pleading insistence. "A solid family structure is important in a child's life. What is taught at home largely determines the way a child reacts to the outside world. Because I couldn't claim my father openly I lost respect for him. I was hostile to the world in general and to my parents in particular. His death shocked me into taking a good, long look at myself, and I didn't like what I saw. I don't want any son or daughter of mine to question their identity, or to someday look at us with resentment and bitterness."

"I understand how you feel, but it would be wrong for us to marry because of the baby. It just wouldn't work, can't you see that, Rob?"

Sharon tensed as strong arms circled her waist, and she suddenly ached with a need to seek peace within his embrace. His hands felt warm and protective against her back, and with a sigh she leaned against him. She thought of the small, sheltering place under her heart where new life was beginning. That tiny person represented an undeniable link with the man who held her with such gentleness, and already her destiny was expanding to include love for her child. Could it also, she wondered breathlessly, open to include love for the child's father?

An impatiently voiced demand broke into her thoughts. "Is that what you think, that I feel obligated to marry you?" When she drew back to look at him, he saw the answer in her eyes. Her doubt fired his emotions, and with a suppressed moan he lowered his mouth and breathed a denial against her lips. "I wanted you before you were carrying my child, Princess."

His sincerity made her confidence blossom, and slowly she circled his neck with her arms. Tentatively she ruffled the thick, wavy hair at his nape, her smile faltering timidly as she noticed his instantaneous reaction. His arms tightened convulsively, and his clear gaze became slumberous with pleasure. As she felt the evidence of his ardor against her, she marveled at her ability to so quickly arouse his masculine hunger.

"Does this feel like I don't want you, Sharon?"

His words proclaimed his intentions as did the desire in his eyes when he looked down at her. She shivered as he again sought her mouth, and she waited with starved impatience to experience the fullness of his kiss. The moment came and passed into memory, and his lips hardened with a masculine insistence that coaxed an excited gasp from her parted lips.

Instantly Rob responded to the betraying sound of her passion, his tongue searching the sweet honey of her mouth as a guttural groan rose from deep inside his body. She felt him shaking beneath the hands that she pressed against his chest. Without hesitation her fingers began an impatient search for satisfaction. Rob's heartbeat accelerated as she pushed aside his jacket and touched him between the buttons of the silky shirt he wore underneath. She sighed her gratification into his open mouth and eagerly released two more buttons until her palms lay flat against his chest.

"Don't stop now," he grunted against her kiss-swollen lips.

He needn't have worried, she thought; her latent sensuality was holding her in a grip too powerful to deny. With unfamiliar aggression the tips of her fingernails scratched a trail through the soft tufts of golden fur covering his chest, finally coming to rest on the small, hardened buds of his masculine nipples. His mouth was against her arched throat and, when he sucked in his breath, she felt the intensity of his desire heat her already molten blood.

"This is insane," she cried softly, her eyes closing as she tried to regain her control.

He nodded, and his teeth nibbled the sensitive flesh underneath her ear. "Deliciously insane, my love."

"My love," she repeated in a whisper. "Those words must be the most beautiful in the world."

"I can think of two others just as lovely."

Rob's hands stilled and were motionless against Sharon's back. She was glad he was now easing their heightened emotions, because she didn't have much confidence in her own ability to stop. This is insane, she thought, but it was such sweet, seductive insanity. She wanted to give in and ride on the tide of his passion. She needed to be swept away from her fear of the future and be reassured by the empathy that had grown between them during the last hour. She needed to let her heart match the joyous rhythm she could feel pounding inside his chest. She needed a warm body to shelter her from life's shadows—she needed Rob!

With a sigh of surrender she wrapped her arms around his waist and rubbed her cheek against his chest. "What words could be more special than 'my love'?"

"My wife," he said quietly.

She tilted her head back and smiled up at him. "My husband sounds even better."

Rob stiffened, his eyes intently watching her face. "Do you mean that, Sharon?"

She ran a caressing hand across his jawline and began tracing his mouth with a teasing finger. "I have a terrific idea, Dr. Barnes."

He smiled with bemused uncertainty. "I'm all ears."

"No you're not," she pouted in mock indignation, "you have quite a few other interesting parts."

"Mmmm, care to tell me your favorite?"

She tilted her head and considered him. "You have a very nice nose, and I'm quite enamored of forceful chins."

He nipped at her marauding finger with strong white teeth and gave her a grin. "I have only one chin, and how can a chin be forceful? When my mouth moves it wobbles." His eyes slid in a sweeping search over her body. "I have a few favorite parts of my own I'd like to tell you about."

She sniffed haughtily and then ruined the effect with a giggle. "Don't you want to hear my idea?"

His brows rose. "Wriggling out of the corner, are you?"

"Well, if you don't want me to spend the night with you, just drop me by my car."

He cupped her face in his hands, his gaze darkening. "Are you serious?"

"Of course I'm serious," she chided gently. "We can stay here tonight, and you can take me to pick up my car in the morning."

"You said you had to work tomorrow. What about a change of clothes?"

"I'll have plenty of time to return home and change," she said.

"Will you hit me over the head if I offer to drive you?"

"What's the alternative?"

"Rope-belted cutoffs and a T-shirt," he stated promptly, adding with a grin, "Although I'm warning you, a shirt with 'Wanna play doctor?' on the back wouldn't impress your clientele."

She laughed in agreement and said, "My staff would love the change, though. They seem to think I do nothing but work."

He looked smug. "That was before you met me. From now on Ms. Vecchio, you are going to learn to play."

She tried to look shocked. "I most certainly am not, Dr. Barnes!"

"You are, too!"

"Am not!"

Rob and Sharon smiled at each other. She took sudden pride in the contentment that filled his eyes and chased away the lines of tension from beside his mouth. She would make him happy, she vowed silently, and reached up to hug him. His grin widened, and as he picked her up and carried her into the bedroom, she knew a precedent had been set in their relationship. Some might call it arguing, she thought happily, but they both knew it was just another way to make love.

Eight

"Robert Barnes, you are not painting the nursery blue!"

Rob grinned and replaced the paint on the store's wide display shelf. "Well, Mrs. Barnes, my son would feel rather out of place with pink walls and ruffled curtains."

"My daughter wouldn't," Sharon declared, her expression bland as she waited for his predictable response.

They had played this game often during the three months they'd been married and it was difficult to decide who enjoyed squabbling the most. They fought over which church to be married in, what flowers Sharon would carry in her bouquet, and whether Rob would wear a suit or a tuxedo for the ceremony. They had argued the merits of a honeymoon location until her sister had taken her aside and hissed into her ear, "Are you crazy? Wait until after the wedding to become temperamental."

Sharon had given Marilyn an innocent stare and managed to keep her expression bland. "Rob might as well know what he's getting."

"But does he have to know everything?" Marilyn had wailed.

Unconsciously Sharon's lip curved into a smile at the memory of her sister's dismay.

"Just what are you smiling about?"

Sharon slanted her husband a glance. "I'm remembering how nervous we made Marilyn at our engagement party."

"She was only edgy until the minister pronounced us man and wife," he reminded her. "She was the life of the party at the reception. If I remember correctly, she was so tipsy Chad and Casey took her home with them."

"It was the relief, darling," she chuckled, twining her arm through his as they continued their exploration of the hardware store's shelves. "She was absolutely sure you were going to take off before I had a chance to shackle you."

"At least Marilyn had the sense to know what a catch you were getting!"

Sharon's lips quivered, but she refused to add to her husband's conceit by giving in to laughter. Instead she pressed a finger against her mouth and gave him a sideways glance. "How about yellow?"

"I beg your pardon?"

"For the baby's room." Sharon patted her rounded tummy and grinned up at him. "You're a little slow today, aren't you?"

He groaned and shook his head in exasperation. "You must be the only woman alive who can carry on two conversations at the same time."

"I am not," she retorted indignantly. "You're just jealous because you aren't quick enough to keep up with me."

Rob immediately took unfair advantage of the situation. His gaze slowly descended to her breasts, which had become fuller as her pregnancy advanced, and his mouth curved with obvious sensuality as he whispered, "Do you really think I can't keep up with you?"

Sharon's cheeks turned as pink as the color she wanted for the nursery. With just a single sentence Rob had reminded her of the way she had turned to wake him as dawn was breaking, still hungry for his lovemaking after the hours already spent in his arms. The memory of how eagerly he'd responded made her eyes glow as she looked at him.

"All right," she muttered, "This round goes to you."

With a smirk of triumph Rob pulled her closer against his side. "I thought it might," he said smugly.

Sharon waggled an admonishing finger in his face. "This is not getting the job done, Dr. Barnes."

"No," he chuckled softly, "I did that this morning."

Sharon dug a sharp elbow into his ribs. "Rob, if you say one more word—"

He stopped walking so suddenly Sharon pitched forward, but he ignored her exasperated glare as he righted her. "What about pale blue walls, fluffy white and pink clouds, with a big fat rainbow in the middle?" he asked, a creative gleam in his eyes.

"What you won't do to get your own way!"

He laughed and tapped her chin with his finger. "Well, what do you think?"

"That you're a genius," she replied with wry emphasis. "What else can I think?"

When they left the air-conditioned comfort of the hardware store, the air hit them with all the subtlety of a blast furnace. While Rob stored their purchases in the trunk of the car, Sharon fanned herself with an inadequate hand. The temperature was well into the eighties, which wasn't at all unusual for September. She and Rob had spent the weekend with Casey and Chad, and just last night Casey had remarked that the real summer weather arrived when school opened. The two women had been sitting on lounge chairs beside the pool, watching as Chad and Rob played with Jonathan in the water.

"Can't we talk you two into staying a few more days?" Casey asked.

Sharon shook her head, her eyes regretful. "I wish we could, but Rob's got the beeper all next week. He'll be on call until next Sunday."

"Couldn't he trade off with one of the other doctors?"

"He could, but he'll be taking time off next month to attend a medical convention in San Francisco. He also has three patients due to deliver, and after doing all the work he insists on being in on the final moments."

"What if they all go into labor at the same time?"

Sharon laughed. "Brilliant minds think alike," she said. "I told him they'll probably do it just to spite him."

"Hey, Mom," a young voice cried, "Uncle Rob taught me how to swim like a fish."

The next several minutes were spent watching Jonathan undulate underwater, his legs held tightly together in lieu of a tail. After praising her son's accomplishment, Casey turned to look at Sharon. "Your husband's a real hit with Jon."

"He's good with children," Sharon said, her voice filled with pride.

"If your fatuous expression is anything to go by," Casey said teasingly, "he's not bad with women, either."

Sharon's face became hot, and it had nothing to do with the outside temperature. "He's passable," she remarked primly.

Casey shouted with laughter. "Oh, Sharon," she managed eventually, wiping her streaming eyes with the back of her hand, "don't ever change. You might irk your sister, but I find you decidedly entertaining."

"Speaking of Marilyn, have you seen her recently?"

"Only at the restaurant," she said.

Sharon's glance shifted to her hands. "She hasn't talked to you about anything?"

"What has she done now?" Casey questioned automatically.

"Why is it," Sharon asked with a grin, "that whenever my sister's name is mentioned we immediately associate her with trouble?"

"Because she manages to get herself into hot water more frequently than anyone else I've ever met," Casey retorted instantly, "and yes, I worked late Friday, and cornered her when she arrived for the dinner shift."

Sharon shrugged with apparent unconcern, but her eyes were worried as she said, "I invited her to stay with us last weekend, but she called at the last minute and canceled."

"There's a new man in her life," Casey admitted with a rueful twist to her lips. "If gossip is to be believed, he's tall, dark and extremely handsome."

"It's not like Marilyn to be secretive."

Casey frowned and nodded. "You're right. She usually can't wait to buttonhole one of us to sing the praises of her latest. I wonder if she's really serious about this guy?''

"Only time will tell," Sharon had replied.

"Are you all right, honey?"

Sharon's reverie was cut short by the worried note in Rob's voice. She blinked, and although she smiled at him reassuringly, her eyes were shadowed by previous thoughts. "I was just worrying about Marilyn."

"Ahh, you found out about her latest."

Sharon's eyes widened with indignation, and she swung around to survey him suspiciously. "You mean she told you about him?"

His expression was complacent. "She wanted my opinion and I gave it to her."

Sharon shook her head. "I practically raised that wretch, and it's you she confides in!"

Rob heard the hurt underlying Sharon's exclamation and placed his arm around her shoulders. "She didn't want to worry you, honey. Your sister's a grown woman and fully capable of handling her affairs."

"That's what I'm afraid of!"

He gave her shoulders a squeeze. "Look, Marilyn and I were talking the last time she visited," he explained. "She mentioned her boyfriend's name, and I asked if he was related to Patricia Boughn."

"And just who is Patricia Boughn?" she asked, jealousy suddenly uppermost in her mind.

"You met Pat a few weeks ago when she dropped in to visit Chad and Casey," he said with a mocking grin. "She's the realtor who helped them buy their house."

She looked sheepish. "The attractive brunette who works for Harris Realty?"

"The very same."

Sharon looked puzzled and tried to remember the last time her sister had visited. "Where was I when this momentous conversation was taking place?"

"You were in the bathroom." He grinned, but when she glared at him he tried to look suitably repentant. "Anyway, you don't have to worry about Marilyn. Unless I miss my guess your sister's swinging single days are nearing an end."

Sharon slumped in relief and muttered fervently, "God willing!"

Rob helped her into the car and was soon beside her in the driver's seat. He leaned forward to help her fasten her seatbelt and dropped a kiss on the tip of her nose. "You're as bad as a brood hen with one chick."

Her spirits immediately lightened and she patted him on the cheek. "Two chicks," she retorted. "I've got you, haven't I?"

"I am not a chick," he remarked stentoriously.

"Are too!"

Rob and Sharon thoroughly enjoyed their discussion which escalated nonsensically during the drive home. They had left later than planned, Casey insisting they stay for lunch before starting out on their return journey. It had been Rob's idea to stop in Dublin for paint, and Sharon was pleasantly tired by the time they reached Sausalito. When they turned into the marina, Sharon's attention was caught by a boat in the distance under full sail.

As they started walking across the wooden dock, Sharon asked, "Isn't that the *Crystal Anne*, Rob?"

He nodded, narrowing his eyes against the glare of the setting sun. "Crystal and Peter must have decided to leave early for the Bahamas."

"The last time I talked to Crystal she said they weren't heading out until the first of October."

"Nothing's ever definite with those two," he laughed. "One minute you see them, the next you don't."

"I wish we could have accepted their invitation to join them," Sharon sighed wistfully.

"Oh, no!" Rob groaned and shifted the paint cans so he had an arm free to hug Sharon to his side. "They'll be gone over two months, and it would be just like you to go into labor early."

"Well," she sniffed, "you're a doctor, aren't you?"

"I'll leave it up to old Larry to deliver my heir," he said with a grimace. "If I had to do the job I'd be so nervous I'd probably drop our son on his head."

"Our daughter," Sharon retorted automatically.

"Our son," he insisted with a grin, "and don't argue or you won't get taken out to dinner."

"Do you call a trip to McDonald's being taken out to dinner?"

"Well, we drive to get there, don't we?"

"I'd rather walk," she insisted, her chin tilted in a warning slant.

"You don't walk, you waddle."

"I do not!"

Sharon was pacing every square inch of the houseboat, muttering beneath her breath as she stared at the closed door between her and the baby's room. "Rob, can I look now?"

"In a minute," he yelled.

"You said that an hour ago," she said, her tone belligerent. "You're not being fair, Robert Barnes. I thought we were going to decorate the nursery together!"

The door opened, and the great creator's face appeared between the crack. "Paint fumes aren't good for you."

Sharon glared at him. "Says who?"

"Says the doctor, Miss Pruneface."

"You're not my doctor!"

He stepped across the threshold and stood facing her. Then he crossed his arms over his chest and tried to look superior. "No, but I am your lord and master."

Her eyes threw sparks at him. "You and who else, buster?"

Rob glanced pointedly at the bulge beneath her gold smock top. "Me and my son."

"Your daughter," she snapped, stamping her foot for emphasis.

Sharon immediately regretted the gesture when Rob's eyes lowered to the carpeted floor. "Have you been sneaking salt behind my back?"

Having a nervous husband when one was pregnant was a trial, she thought, but when he was a doctor as well, a girl didn't stand a chance. She threw her head back, her expression defiant. "I ate one lousy potato chip, Rob!"

He moved forward and gripped her shoulders. "I'm not trying to play Mr. Macho," he said, his eyes mirroring his concern, "but I don't like the way your feet and legs are swelling, Sharon. You could be heading for toxemia."

Sharon's smile was wry, her expression apologetic. "I don't much like it, either. I'm already wearing your sandals since none of my shoes fit me."

"Mmmm, don't worry about appearances," he murmured, sliding his hands up and down her arms. "I've got a fetish for toes."

"You've got a fetish for big stomachs, too, or you wouldn't say good-night to mine every night!"

His laugh vibrated the cheek she had pressed to his chest. "By the time that little bruiser comes into the world he'll recognize the sound of his father's voice."

Her smile was hidden against his paint-splattered shirt. "Then you can get up for the two o'clock feeding and talk him back to sleep."

"You said he," he said, his expression reflecting his satisfaction.

She mumbled a rude word beneath her breath. "A mere slip of the tongue, but since we're on the subject, when can I view your masterpiece?" she asked, with barely restrained impatience.

"Give me a kiss and I'll let you take a peek."

Sharon drew back, her eyes gleaming wickedly as she looked up at him. "A little kiss," she asked with assumed innocence, "or a big kiss?"

He cleared his throat, his attention caught by the pink tongue tip Sharon was using to moisten her lips. His voice was husky as he suggested, "Why don't we play it by ear?"

Sharon played it for all she was worth. Reaching up to pull his head down to hers, she nibbled at his lower lip until she heard him gasp. Then she slowly rocked her body against his and opened her mouth so he could engage her exploring tongue in a sensual duel. By the time she pulled away she was having every bit as much trouble drawing a decent breath as Rob was.

"You can look at the decor later," he muttered, beginning to edge her toward their bedroom. "We can take a nap while the room airs out."

Sharon knew her curiosity would return eventually, but at the moment all she could think about was the quickest way to get the hot-eyed male in front of her out of his clothes. She didn't have to wonder long because Rob took matters into his own hands. In an amazingly short span of time they were both sprawled on top of their bed, each luxuriating in the closeness of the other.

Sharon heard the hypnotic lapping of water against the houseboat and smiled as Rob's fingers spread over her stomach in a possessive gesture. She marveled at her lack of self-consciousness and knew he sincerely meant the words of praise he was whispering against her breast. When his lips gently encircled her nipple, the words were silenced, but Sharon needed no encouragement to know she was desired. Her fingers stroked the evidence, her smile widening when Rob growled a warning.

"I thought you liked me to touch you?" she murmured teasingly.

"Like is too mild a word, my love," he groaned, turning her on her side until her back was warmed by his chest.

Sharon sucked in a breath as she guessed his intent and twisted her head around until their mouths met. Her husband's tender concern for her never failed to arouse her. She felt as though she were drowning in sensation and eagerly complied with Rob's silent manipulation as he guided her leg to a resting place on top of his hip. Her passion had peaked with unbelievable swiftness, and as she felt herself opening to the thrust of his male body she knew, with a sense of wonder, that she had never been happier.

After the heat of their ardor had subsided, Sharon nestled contentedly in her husband's arms. The screened window opposite the bed was open, and a slight breeze cooled their bodies as they talked quietly together.

"Have I told you how much I love you today?"

Sharon pressed a kiss against his throat. "Didn't you just show me?"

"Mmmm, I'm always surprised when we make love."

She lifted up on her elbow and searched his eyes. "Surprised?"

With studied tenderness Rob brushed a damp tendril of hair from her temple. "I think it can't ever get better, yet each time with you is like the first."

"For me, too," she whispered, her eyes glowing with contentment as she bent to brush a kiss against his mouth. "I lose all touch with reality when we make love, as though I only exist through you. It's a little frightening."

He ran his hand across her smooth shoulder. "I know what you mean," he said, after a slight hesitation. "Everything else fades into insignificance when we're together like this. I wanted a woman with integrity and generosity who would give herself to me without holding anything back. After years of searching, you walked into my life. I'm a very lucky man, Princess."

Sharon hid her sudden frown against his neck while she struggled against an urge to silence his words. He wanted a woman with integrity, she thought in anguish, and what he got was someone who had been living a lie from the moment they'd met. Why had she ever gone to that damn clinic? Why hadn't she told him the truth in the beginning? Oh, God...what if he ever found out?

Her heart began to race, and she took several deep breaths to calm herself. He can't find out, she reassured herself silently. You called the clinic and let them know you were no longer interested in artificial insemination. The woman you spoke to promised to take your name from the waiting list. But a nagging voice inside her head gained precedence over her thoughts— *You should tell him, Sharon.* She pressed closer to Rob's warmth and drew comfort from his body.

"Hey, are you trying to do a Dracula number on my neck, woman?"

Sharon choked on a laugh and prayed Rob wouldn't hear the hint of tears in her voice when she whispered, "Sometimes I put my hands on my stomach and tell our baby how pleased he's going to be with his father."

He tilted her chin back against his arm and gazed down at her. "And are you pleased with his father?"

This time she couldn't halt the tears that filled her eyes. "I am very pleased with his father."

Rob's breath escaped with a sigh and then he rolled onto his side until they faced each other on the pillow. He grinned, attempting to lighten the serious mood that had overtaken them both. "You said 'he' again," he reminded her softly.

"Another slip of the tongue," she said with an answering smile. "Pay no attention."

At that moment a disconcerted expression crossed her features, and she glanced down at her midsection in surprise. "The little devil just kicked me," she said in awestruck tones.

"You try calling me 'she,'" he laughed, "and see what you get."

Sharon shoved a fist into his ribs and smiled with satisfaction when he groaned. "Maybe it was you our daughter was trying to kick."

He patted her tummy, his eyes alight with mischievous delight. "Do you think we disturbed our infant's rest?"

Sharon flushed, and a tiny smile played across her lips as she began to trace his jaw with an impudent finger. "Well, since she's already awake, why don't we...?"

Her voice trailed into significant silence, and when she peeked at Rob through her lashes she saw the incredulous delight in his eyes. "Are you planning on early widowhood, woman?"

"I thought you could keep up with me?" she pouted.

Rob chuckled as he slid his hand over her bottom and pulled her forcibly against his hips. "Just watch me try, my love!"

Since Sharon had issued the challenge she couldn't blame Rob when she dozed off and didn't wake up until four o'clock. There was a silly smile playing at the corners of her mouth as she showered and donned a frilly green-and-cream smock top. She had a little difficulty getting into the slacks with the wide band of elastic in the front, but it was no fault of the manufacturer. The problem was with her feet, which she couldn't see, and with her waist, which she couldn't bend.

The task was eventually completed with much huffing and puffing, and Sharon wondered if other mothers-to-be had this much trouble by the time they were almost six months along. Maybe some, she thought, but not all. She felt as swollen and unattractive as a beached whale, and even that simile was stretching a point. Her mouth twisted, acknowledging the unintended pun, then she went in search of Rob. Being with him would put her in a happier frame of mind.

Their houseboat was wide and level, and it didn't take her long to realize he was nowhere to be found. She tapped on the door of the nursery. When Rob didn't answer she passed through the hall and entered the living room. She stepped onto the small deck that served in lieu of a patio, glad she'd been able to resist the temptation to take a peek at the baby's room. She wanted to wait for Rob.

The breeze was brisk as she stood beside the railing and looked across at the other boats moored nearby. The day was clear, and she shaded her eyes to avoid the glare of the sinking sun reflected off the water. As she had suspected, Rob was standing in the bow of a nearby yacht talking animatedly with the newcomer.

She saw her husband gesture toward the horizon and smiled. With Rob around, the owners of the sleek teak-and-brass beauty wouldn't remain unknown for long.

As he'd promised, her husband had taught her to play. He was a gregarious creature who loved to mingle with his friends. At first Sharon had felt uncomfortable attending the various social gatherings the yacht club provided, but she hadn't been allowed to be uneasy for long. Rob had kept her at his side until she knew enough of the female members to feel a part of the festivities. Her relationship with Rob had given her a self-confidence she'd never had before, and she had been amazed at how easily she made friends.

Sharon turned, her thoughts on the roast she planned to cook for dinner. When she entered the kitchen she saw a note pinned to the refrigerator. "If you've sneaked a look at our son's room," she read out loud, "I'm going to make you double your exercises this evening. I won't be long...Love, Rob."

She laughed and shook her head. Whenever that husband of hers planned a surprise he was like a small child eager to earn praise for his efforts. And she loved him, she thought wonderingly. She loved him more with each day that passed. She didn't know when Michael's image had been supplanted by Rob's in her heart, but she suspected it had happened on the night their child was conceived. She had tried to deny what she was feeling by running away, and she trembled when she realized how close she'd come to never experiencing her present happiness.

Sharon was amazed at how easily she'd adapted to married life. She'd given up her apartment without a moment's regret, and notified the Post Office to forward her mail to her new address. Once the practicalities had been taken care of, she thought with a grin, she and Rob had begun living together with admirable expertise.

She heard Rob's firm stride while she was lifting the roast from the oven. The table was already set with the ceramic dishes she'd brought from her apartment. Except for a couple of easy chairs, the rest of her furniture was being stored until Rob's beach house was completed. Because he wanted his family to have a weekend retreat as soon as possible, Rob had hired a firm of contractors to do the alterations. He didn't seem to mind not doing the restoration himself as he had first planned. He was too busy learning to be a husband.

Sharon finished slicing the roast and arranged the potatoes and carrots in an attractive circle on the platter. She placed her masterpiece on the table and yelled for Rob, nearly jumping out of her skin when he grabbed what was left of her waist from behind.

"Mmmm, you smell good enough to eat," he said, nuzzling the back of her neck.

"That's the oil I rubbed on my stomach."

He bit the lobe of her ear. "Hey, that's not fair," he protested with a laugh. "You know that's my favorite chore."

"Will you stop kissing my neck and sit down before our meal gets cold?"

He held out her chair for her and sat down at the opposite end of the table. "Am I in trouble?"

She gestured to the note on the refrigerator door and tried not to laugh at his chagrined expression. "I don't respond well to threats, Robert Barnes."

His eyes rounded in surprise. "Then what do you respond to, angel face?"

"A gentlemanly suggestion would have sufficed," she replied with a pout, "or you could have tried bribing me." She placed her elbow on the table and cupped her chin in her hand. "I need a new winter coat."

A sliver of meat was transferred from Rob's fork to his mouth. He watched her while he chewed, his expression thoughtful. "You really liked the one in the boutique window, didn't you?"

"Oh, yes," she sighed. "It was the most elegant thing I've ever seen." Then she grimaced and looked down at herself in disgust. "It wouldn't fit now, anyway."

His mouth quirked, but he said in all seriousness, "You won't be pregnant for much longer."

"Three months seems like forever," she admitted wryly, beginning to eat without enthusiasm. "By the time the baby is born all the stores will be stocking summer clothes.''

Rob got to his feet and patted her on the shoulder as he passed her chair. "Keep your chin up, darling," he advised. "I'll be back in a minute."

"I might as well," she responded glumly. "It doesn't do me a bit of good to look down when I can't even see my own feet." She was still engulfed in her bout of self-pity when something warm and soft was placed around her shoulders. "My coat," she whispered, rubbing her cheek against the fur collar.

"I was going to save it until after the baby was born," he said quietly, "but I think you need it more now."

There were tears in her eyes as she lifted her face. "Oh, Rob," she whispered, her mouth trembling, "you must be the best husband in the world."

"Since I'm not guilty of false modesty," he said with a grin, "I'll agree with you."

He kissed her lingeringly and then moved to slip the coat from her shoulders. "What are you doing?" she squealed, grabbing at his hand.

"I'm just going to hang it up in the closet while you finish dinner."

She transferred her grip to the fur and shook her head. "Oh, no you're not," she insisted, laughter provocatively curving her mouth. "I'm going to wear it while I eat, and when we take our walk this evening, and..."

His eyes narrowed with suspicion as he interrupted. "Just where else do you plan to wear the darned thing, Mrs. Barnes?"

She chuckled and gave his cheek a reassuring pat. "Why, to bed of—"

Before the sentence could be completed he was shaking his head. "Oh, no, you're not!"

She tilted her chin pugnaciously while her eyes sparkled with glee. "I am, too!"

"Are not!"

The coat remained draped against Sharon's back while they finished their meal. It was still being worn when they rinsed the plates and cutlery and loaded them into the dishwasher. Later, when they took their evening walk, she luxuriated in its warmth. But by the time darkness fell she remembered to compromise. When she went to bed all that covered her was a blue satin spread and her husband's strong, comforting arms.

Nine

Sharon was looking glumly out of the window as she talked to Casey on the phone. Rain was dripping down the glass, and the sky was so dark with angry clouds that the stars were totally obscured. The weather suited her mood, she thought, as she pressed her free hand against the small of her back. Her back ached because she'd been standing too long, but then so did her swollen feet, her swollen legs and her swollen tummy.

Come to think of it, she was just as miserable sitting down as standing up. Her decision made, she reached for a kitchen chair and plopped onto it with a relieved groan. A cushiony armchair would be more comfortable, she thought with a frown, but she'd never be able to get up on her own. Without a doubt her entire body felt as though it had been squeezed through a wringer and hung out to dry.

"Sharon, are you in pain?"

Casey's shriek added ears to Sharon's list of things that hurt. "Of course I'm not, you idiot. Why should I be?"

"You could be going into labor for all I know!"

"I wouldn't dare start this baby without Rob," Sharon muttered. "It took me long enough to talk him into attending this conference, and he only agreed to go after I promised not to jump the gun."

Sharon knew she was complaining but she was past caring. As much as she'd wanted to have this child, she hadn't realized what she was letting herself in for. She was watched and poked, prodded and scolded, until she was in danger of forgetting what normal felt like.

"Sharon, maybe you'd better go and lie down," Casey suggested.

"Don't you start," Sharon snapped petulantly. "Do you know Rob actually had the nerve to dump the salt in the sink before he left this morning?"

"What a rotten thing to do!"

Sharon held the receiver in front of her face and glared at it. She was almost sure she'd heard a trace of amusement in Casey's voice but decided to let it pass. She glanced at her watch and cheered up a little when she noted the time. The medical convention Rob had been attending all week concluded tonight. She was glad the darn meetings were finally over. She had missed their evenings together.

Casey said a cheerful goodbye and Sharon replaced the receiver with a scowl. "At least one of us can find something to be cheerful about," she mumbled. Then she tried to remember if her voice had been just a touch whiny when she had complained about the salt. She hated whiny pregnant women! She pushed herself out of the chair with a moan and wondered if all pregnant women whined a little. Not me, she told herself bracingly. I never whine!

Keeping that positive thought in mind, she took a refreshing shower and put on her favorite maternity dress. The material was crushed velvet in a lovely shade of teal blue. That it was Rob's favorite color had been taken into consideration.

She'd just finished with her makeup and was spraying her wrists with perfume when she heard her husband's voice calling her name. She smiled as a swift dart of excitement caused her heart to pound. It was positively indecent for a woman seven months pregnant to act so eager, she decided with a laugh, but the thought didn't stop her as she rushed to greet him.

He was standing with his back to her when she entered the room, and she moved forward to circle his waist from behind. "It's about time you got home, doctor," she said as she hugged him. "I've missed you."

"Have you?"

Rob's voice sounded odd, and Sharon drew back with a puzzled frown. "Is something wrong, Rob?"

He turned to face her, and she caught her breath at the paleness of his features. He lifted his hand with pointed emphasis, and Sharon lowered her gaze to the mail he held in his hand. She returned her worried gaze to his face. "I don't know what you're trying to tell me, Rob. Have you received some bad news?"

His mouth twisted. "You might say that." He selected a paper from the several he held and gave it to her. "I think if you read this it might clarify matters."

Sharon glanced down at the letter and felt the blood drain from her face. It was from the Oakland clinic, and being a doctor Rob would be well aware of the main function of this particular medical facility. As though that weren't damning enough, the sight of her own name accompanied by the date of her visit was typed with a clarity that made it seem like an accusation. Oh, God! she thought in stunned realization. She had called to have her name removed from a list of prospective patients, but had completely forgotten about the advance payment she'd given them. The letter had been forwarded from her former landlord.

As though to corroborate this Rob said, "I saw the clinic address and assumed the letter was for me." He held out the envelope. "There's a check inside made out to you, minus their charge for the consultation visit."

"Rob, please let me explain."

"You told me how badly you wanted this child, Sharon." He laughed harshly and looked at her disbelievingly. "I must have misinterpreted your meaning."

Sharon saw the pain Rob didn't try to hide and lifted her hand in a placating gesture. "Rob, I—"

She was immediately interrupted. "You don't have to play the loving wife any longer, Sharon. I'm only sorry you thought you needed to pander to my masculine ego in the first place. You should have explained your desire for single parenthood," he said coldly. "I wanted you pretty badly at the time. Who knows? I might have thrown my principles aside, and then you wouldn't have felt you had to marry me."

"Rob, wait," she cried, as he began to move past her. "You don't understand."

"Understand what?" he asked quietly, his eyes inspecting Sharon's ashen features with almost clinical detachment. "Understand that you were too impatient to wait? That you used me to get what you wanted?"

"I didn't mean—"

"I know you didn't intend for me to find out, Sharon. Believe me, I would have much preferred to continue living in a fool's paradise, but the damage is done."

"I know I should have told you about my plans to undergo artificial insemination, but I just couldn't," she said in a trembling voice. "I knew how it would appear to you and I couldn't bear to have our relationship harmed in any way."

He winced and gestured her to silence. "Please," he said softly, his voice devoid of emotion as he walked past her, "spare me any more lies. I don't think I could stomach them right now."

Rob continued down the hall and entered their bedroom. Sharon heard the door close behind him and felt as though she'd been shut away from the happiness she'd only recently learned to believe in. Yet, in a way she almost felt relieved that she no longer had anything to hide. She'd been carrying the guilt around inside of her, and now that her worst fears were realized she could openly bring it forth and look at it.

She knew she had only herself to blame for the situation in which she now found herself. If only she'd told Rob about visiting the sperm bank when they had talked together on the beach! So much misery and pain could have been averted. Yet wasn't hindsight always easier than foresight?

She wasn't a complete washout as a human being because of one lapse, but that wasn't the issue in question. Rob had believed in her strength of character, her basic honesty in their relationship. She had encouraged that belief and in doing so had given less to their marriage than she should have. Was it any wonder, she realized painfully, that his pride had suffered? Wouldn't anyone, given the same set of circumstances, feel used and degraded?

Now she was going to pay for her silence by losing the respect she prized so highly. Just one glance at his expression had been enough to show her his trust in her was gone. She couldn't think of a way to mend the trouble her deceit had caused. All she did understand was the necessity to try—to somehow convince Rob he was so much more to her than just a father for her child.

Sharon drew out her nightly chores, her heart pounding with nervous dread as she tried to summon the courage to face her husband. She wanted to be in control herself, but after hesitating by the bedroom door for the third time she knew she couldn't wait any longer. She was about as composed as she was ever going to be, she thought as she reached for the handle on the door. Taking a deep breath she pulled it open and stepped into the room before she had a chance to change her mind.

It took her a full minute to accept what she saw when she switched on the overhead light. Rob was sprawled on his stomach, his eyes closed while he breathed with rhythmic regularity. Her first reaction was one of incredulity, which rapidly escalated into indignation. How could he have fallen asleep with so much discord between them? she asked herself. She walked toward the bed with every intention of waking him up so they could talk, but paused before her hand reached his shoulder.

He looks exhausted, she thought. Her second thought was far more distressful as she took note of an unusual degree of restlessness in his body. While she watched, a muscle in his back throbbed spasmodically and his head twisted against the pillow as though he unconsciously searched for a more comfortable resting place. He appeared to be having a nightmare, and when he moaned her name she felt her eyes fill with helpless tears.

Sharon knew it would do no good to wake him since she was the cause of his distress. There was a defeated slump to her shoulders as she lowered her hand to her side and turned to leave the room. She hesitated briefly before depressing the light switch, but she needn't have bothered delaying the inevitable, she thought tiredly. When she looked back at Rob she knew the darkness of the room was no more deprived of light than her heart.

Sharon was jolted from a fitful doze by the ringing of the telephone. The afghan covering her slid to the floor beside the couch, and she stared groggily around the room as she slowly remembered why she hadn't gone to bed. When the ringing stopped she realized Rob must have lifted the bedroom extension. With a groan she lay back and covered her burning eyes with an outflung arm.

"What are you doing out here?"

She jumped at the sound of Rob's voice and slowly uncovered her eyes. The weak light of early morning cast his face in shadow, but there was enough illumination for Sharon to see the unaccustomed hardness of his expression. Lifting herself up on her elbow she attempted a weak smile. "I don't really know," she said. "I was sitting here last night trying to think of a way to explain everything to you. I guess I must have fallen asleep."

"Why don't you just admit the truth," he asked, his voice expressionless. "I assure you I can take it."

"The truth?" she questioned, cursing her own stupidity as she failed to make sense of his remark. "What are you talking about?"

"Since I've already provided you with what you wanted," he said, his glance dropping with pointed emphasis to her rounded stomach, "there's no need to humor me any longer by sharing my bed. Isn't that why you're sleeping on the couch?"

"That's nonsense," she exclaimed hurriedly. "I knew I was pregnant when we married, and I've never refused to sleep with you, Rob."

"Because you knew how I felt about you and couldn't bring yourself to disillusion me."

Sharon gasped at the enormity of his misconception. "You can't really believe that!"

Rob shook his head in an attitude of defeat and leaned his bare shoulder against the wall. He wore only pajama bottoms, and the rippling muscles in his arms caused her to swallow convulsively. "I don't have time to go into this now," he said abruptly. "One of my patients is in labor."

"Rob, I want to know what you—"

Sharon's words stopped as Rob's hand sliced through the air, his impatience marked as he said, "We'll discuss our situation later, Sharon. Right now I have to get to the hospital."

The day passed with agonizing slowness as Sharon tried to occupy herself until Rob got home. She cleaned the houseboat from top to bottom and ignored her flagging energy as she struggled to keep herself too busy to think. But no matter how hard she tried she couldn't help remembering Rob's promise to discuss their situation. The way he expressed himself had sounded ominous, she thought, as though he had already made up his mind about the direction such a discussion would take.

Dinner that evening was fraught with tension, and only desultory conversation took place between Sharon and Rob. Although Sharon ached to explain her reasons for not confiding in Rob about her appointment with the sperm bank, her husband's manner was distant enough to convince her to contain her impatience. She decided that if she tried to force the issue he would most likely think she was on the defensive. She didn't want to do anything to weaken her position any further, or to give Rob more reason to distrust her.

With a distant manner Rob took over the chore of cleaning the kitchen and she had no choice but to wander alone into the living room. Seating herself in a high-backed wing chair that eased the ache in her spine, she took up her discarded knitting to give herself something to do. Yet she was unable to concentrate on the pattern for the tiny sweater. Her eyes constantly lifted to watch her husband as he moved about the other room.

Although she was relieved when Rob finished his tasks and joined her in the living room, she felt almost sick with nervous tension. When he reached for the paper on top of the metal stand beside the couch and sat down to read, she stared across at him in amazed comprehension. Even though his face was hidden from her view, she'd caught a brief glimpse of the implacable set to his mouth, realizing that he didn't intend to talk to her.

Sharon put her knitting aside, straightened her back and readied herself for a confrontation. Nothing was going to be accomplished with both of them sitting in the same room like a couple of zombies. Even though she was guilty of duplicity, she was being judged without a hearing. She was damned if she was just going to let him condemn her.

"Rob, I think it's time you explained what you meant when you left for the hospital this morning."

The paper was refolded and replaced in the magazine rack, and the face Rob turned to her showed little expression. "You mean when I said we'd discuss our situation?"

Well, at least he's had the subject on his mind, she thought, trying to curb her resentment. As a result her nod was stilted, but her eyes still showed her trepidation. "Yes," she agreed, moistening her dry mouth with the tip of her tongue. "You sounded quite cryptic. If you meant you wanted to discuss our marriage, why didn't you say so?"

"Our marriage," he repeated almost indifferently. "By all means let's discuss our marriage."

Sharon's features expressed the pain she was feeling. "Rob, you've drawn the wrong conclusion. Won't you let me explain?"

He nodded, and Sharon rushed into speech. She talked about the emptiness of her life before they met and her certainty that no man could ever replace Michael. Then she expressed her desire to have a child while she was physically able, finishing with, "I had to make a decision, Rob. I'd just returned from that consultation appointment with the sperm bank in Oakland, and was trying to come to terms with the difficulties I would face when my child started asking questions about his or her father.''

A muscle in Rob's cheek twitched as he struggled to control his reaction. ''Then it was lucky you and I met when we did, Sharon. All your problems were solved by a romp in the sheets.''

''It wasn't like that,'' she exclaimed, twisting her hands together in her lap. ''When I first saw you every other consideration left my mind.''

''You mean you saw me and stopped worrying about the pros and cons of single parenthood?'' He laughed, and there wasn't a trace of amusement in his eyes. ''I just bet you did!''

The anger Sharon had been trying to control was fanned into life by Rob's deliberate attempt to antagonize her. ''Just what are you implying by that?''

''If I take the time to refresh your memory, I think you'll be able to see my point of view, Sharon.''

He sat forward on the edge of the couch and rested his elbows on his knees. He didn't look in her direction as he began to speak, but kept his gaze lowered to the carpet. ''We talked a lot that first night we were together, yet not once did you give me any details of your life or encourage me to speak of mine. When you were ready to leave I offered to walk with you, and you told me you didn't live far,'' he said, briefly pinioning her with a glance. ''That was your first lie, Sharon.''

"I was confused, and frightened by my attraction to you."

"Is that why you asked me not to spoil it?" he asked with a pained smile. "How would my knowing where you lived spoil anything, unless you had your own reasons for keeping me in ignorance?"

"I didn't know you," she stammered.

"Yet shortly thereafter you trusted me enough to accept an invitation to my beach house." His brow lifted in a cynical arch. "I still didn't know your full name, nor you mine, when you let me take you to bed."

"You know that wasn't planned," she murmured shakily.

"I think it was planned only too well, Sharon. I think you decided to get pregnant by more conventional means and you used me. You left without a word of farewell the next morning, secure in the knowledge that you might be pregnant. You had no intention of ever coming back unless, of course," he corrected bitterly, "our sexual encounter failed to have the desired result. In that case I suppose you might have looked me up again."

Sharon's eyes widened in horror. "That's not true!"

"Truth or a lie," he said tiredly, "what difference does it make?"

Sharon ground her teeth together, frustrated by his attempt to provoke her. "I had no ulterior motive in going to bed with you, Rob."

He ran his hand through his hair, his fingers tumbling the golden locks into disarray. "God, I'd like to believe you, Sharon."

Getting to her feet she joined him on the couch. "You've got to believe me!" She rested her forehead against his arm and mumbled anxiously, "I swear I didn't consciously plan to use you."

He heard the emotion cracking her voice and leaned against the back of the couch. With the gentleness she had come to expect from him he drew her closer to his side, and she lifted her face to study his expression. There were deep lines tightening his mouth, and her heart ached from the unhappiness she was causing him. "If all I'd wanted was a baby, then why do you think I married you?"

Sharon waited tensely for his reply, her heart beating so fast she felt suffocated. So much depended on his answer. Her hand moved restlessly against his chest as she stared at him.

Slowly he turned his head and looked down at her with a shuttered gaze. "I told you what I thought this morning, but I guess I didn't make myself understood."

"Then maybe it's time you did, Rob."

"When we met again at the clinic I jumped to certain conclusions," he admitted quietly. "I took it for granted you would want to marry me since you were already carrying my child. Even when you balked at the idea I wasn't smart enough to catch your drift. Hell," he muttered gratingly, "I acted like a besotted idiot and you took pity on me, Sharon. That's why you married me, because you're too softhearted to deliberately cause anyone pain.''

"Oh Rob!" she exclaimed brokenly, resisting the urge to clutch at him when he removed his arm from around her shoulders and got to his feet. "You're so wrong!"

"Then why haven't you ever told me you loved me, Sharon?"

His back was to her as he whispered the question so he didn't see the color recede from her face. She tried to answer him, yet she couldn't force the words from her throat. She had no defense, she realized, a feeling of hopelessness keeping her mute. Although she remembered the many times she'd mentally admitted her love for Rob, her natural reserve and shyness had prevented the openness she'd so often craved.

The silence dragged on until he made a move to leave her, and fright gave her the impetus she needed. With a stifled gasp she rushed toward him and wrapped her arms around his waist. "I do love you," she insisted, pressing her cheek against his rigidly held back. "I love you so much, Rob! Please," she whispered, her voice husky with emotion, "please believe me, darling. I have no reason to lie to you, not now when you know everything."

Rob turned unexpectedly and took hold of her shoulders. He steadied her when she stumbled, and his hand moved to her face. Her head was tilted back until he could see her expression. It was then he saw the tears that ran in rivulets down her ashen cheeks. A muscle pulsed in his jaw, and he opened his mouth with a groan. "Don't cry, Sharon."

"We've been happy together, Rob." As she spoke she forced him closer by placing her arms around his neck and closed her eyes to shut out the sight of his uncompromising expression. "If you won't believe I loved you when we married, can you at least accept the fact that I love you now?"

There was a marked silence while Sharon held her breath and then with a moan Rob lowered his mouth to her throat. "Tell me you want me," he demanded.

Sharon searched for his parted lips and sighed her response. "I love you."

His eyes were hotly aroused as he looked at her. "Tell me you want me, Sharon!"

"I want you, Rob."

Again he bent over her, his mouth and hands robbing her of coherent thought as she responded blindly to his masculine need. His face appeared almost driven as he lifted her in his arms and carried her through to their darkened bedroom. His intensity was strangely frightening, but she made no protest when he undressed her and then himself with less than his usual finesse. His body was hard, his flesh warm as he joined her on the bed.

Sharon tried to show Rob what she felt for him through the responsiveness of her body. She arched against the lips that hungrily sought her breasts. Her head twisted restlessly against the pillow, her hips rising and falling in the evocative rhythm of desire. The tips of her fingers seemed sensitized as they trailed restlessly over his perspiration-dampened flesh, her thoughts anticipating the moment Rob would release her from a torrent of longing.

Yet he continued to hold himself aloof. Finally she stiffened, her body on the verge of explosive response. "Rob, please, I can't wait any longer," she whimpered.

His voice was harsh when he asked, "Do you need me?"

She sobbed, "You know I do!"

Sharon was unprepared for the climax that left her shuddering. She wasn't even aware that Rob had finally allowed himself to follow her into a realm of pleasure where two should become one.

Rob silently curved her pliant body against his, his arm a possessive weight around her as he slept. She felt the regular rhythm of his breathing against her back and tensed with resentment. In trying to convince him of her love she'd been deprived of her pride, she thought bitterly. Rob had locked himself away from her.

Ten

Sharon was awakened the next morning by the sound of the shower and lay lethargically with the blankets drawn up around her neck. She felt depleted of energy in both body and spirit as she remembered how she had tried to reach across the barrier of Rob's mistrust . . . and failed. He had listened to words of want and need and closed his heart to those of love. As a result she felt unable to cope with the start of a new day and wanted nothing more than to return to sleep. She didn't want to think, and she certainly couldn't stand the idea of facing Rob across the breakfast table as though nothing had happened.

With mute desperation she pushed the thought aside while her eyes searched for a distraction. Her attention was caught by a pile of clothing thrown carelessly over the back of her dressing table chair. Some distraction, she thought sickly. They were her clothes and Rob's, their wrinkled state a vivid reminder of the hurried manner in which they had been discarded. As though to taunt her a vision of Rob's face leaped into her mind. She winced from the memory of his passion, because she had known then with a deep, wounding certainty, that she had been unable to reach past the barrier he had placed between them.

Sharon touched the pulse pounding against her temple with a languid hand. The air she drew into her lungs was unsatisfying, and she felt stifled in the closed room. As though searching for escape her eyes were drawn to the window. The cream draperies were slightly parted, and she noticed the gray, overcast skies. The hot summer nights spent in Rob's arms were in the past, but it didn't matter. How could it, when winter had already lodged in her heart?

The noise from the shower ceased, and Sharon quickly closed her eyes. Shivering, she burrowed her face into the pillow and raised the blankets higher around her neck. When Rob entered the room his footsteps were muffled by the thick carpet, yet she was aware of the exact instant he paused by the foot of their bed. She tried to breathe evenly, although the acceleration of her pulse made the effort close to impossible. When he turned to collect clean clothing from the closet, her relief was so palpable she nearly groaned out loud.

Eventually Rob halted in front of the mirror above the dresser, and Sharon couldn't resist the temptation to study him surreptitiously as he ran a brush through his hair. His virile physique was emphasized by a pair of black slacks that tightly molded his frame. Slowly her gaze traveled upward, and she caught her breath. She was painfully conscious of every aspect of his lean, well-proportioned body, as though he had tapped the deepest resources of a sensuality she'd been unaware existed within herself.

"Are you going to lie there and pretend to be asleep until I leave, Sharon?"

Although the question was uttered quietly, she jumped in surprise. Closing her eyes again would be nearly as childish as faking sleep had been in the first place, she thought, and yet she couldn't bring herself to reply. Before she had a chance to think she turned her back to him, her body rigid with rejection.

Her teeth were clamped tightly together as she heard Rob approach the bed. She could feel the intensity of his gaze, her senses acutely heightened by his closeness. When the mattress gave way beneath his weight, she gripped the edge of the sheet and blankets until her fingers felt numb. "I don't think you need me to wish you a fond farewell," she said tiredly. "You wouldn't believe me, anyway."

She heard the irritation in his voice as he said, "Don't act like a child, Sharon."

She hesitated before she rolled over onto her back, needing a private moment to steel herself against showing her feelings. "Aren't you going to be late for work?"

"Sharon, look at me."

The request proved irresistible, and her lashes fluttered upward. Instantly she felt overwhelmed by the attraction just the sight of him could elicit from her.

When his gaze followed the movement of her tongue as it slid along her mouth, she felt no satisfaction in knowing he was as helpless as she to withstand the desire that always coursed between them. She was ashamed of her inability to stem the craving in her body for his touch and frightened that he would see the weakness she was trying so desperately to hide.

"Do you want me to fix breakfast?"

He straightened, and the hand that had moved to touch her fell to his side. "I don't have time," he said, his words abrupt. "Because of the convention I'm going to have a lot of work to catch up on, so I might as well get an early start."

"Will you be home for dinner?"

He frowned at the apathy in her voice but didn't remark on her attitude. He merely replied, "As long as you don't mind putting our meal back a couple of hours."

"Will eight-thirty be all right?"

"Fine," he said briefly. "Will you be okay on your own? I could call Frank Sheldon's wife and ask her to come over and keep you company until I get home."

Her laugh sounded slightly hysterical, but she faced him proudly. "Of course I'm all right," she insisted with an edge of anger lacing her voice. "Since when have I become too feebleminded to take care of myself?''

"Since when have you become so sarcastic?'' he countered.

She shrugged, and her mouth tightened defensively. "Everyone changes, given time.''

He ran a hand through his hair, his eyes disturbed. "Look, I don't like leaving when I know you're upset. We need to talk—''

Sharon shook her head, the gesture effectively halting Rob's statement. "All I need right now is a little more sleep,'' she said, turning her eyes away from him.

"Refusing to speak to me isn't going to solve our problems, Sharon.''

"I spoke to you last night, but you didn't believe a word I said,'' she reminded him, her expression conveying a bitterness she didn't try to stem. "I can't stop you from thinking I'm lying to you, but I'm damned if I'm going to carry all the blame for the deterioration of our relationship. As far as I'm concerned,'' she concluded angrily, "you evened the score last night.''

"What in hell are you talking about?''

"I used you,'' she exclaimed defiantly, "and you used me. Doesn't that make us even?''

She had wanted to hurt him, and she succeeded with the lie. His face suddenly paled, and he rose tiredly to his feet. "Well, I wanted the truth.''

"You wouldn't recognize the truth if it hit you between the eyes,'' she choked, her eyes shimmering with unshed tears.

"Just as you didn't, Sharon?"

She averted her face and plucked small pieces of fuzz off the wool blanket with nervous fingers. "I don't know what you mean."

He leaned forward and placed his hands on either side of her head. "You know very well what I mean," he whispered, the intensity of his gaze forcing her attention. "Last night I tried to shut you out, Sharon. The fact that I was disturbed by our conversation is no excuse. Telling you I'm sorry isn't going to change anything."

Hearing Rob try to categorize what had happened between them caused the blood to drain from her face. "You made me feel so alone," she whispered. "Do you hate me now, Rob?"

He groaned and drew her into his arms. "You little fool, of course I don't hate you," he said, sounding shaken. "It's myself I'm hating."

Sharon frowned and moved restlessly against his tightening arms. "What do you mean?"

Rob eased her back onto the pillow and got to his feet. As he noticed the wariness of her expression his own features showed both pain and remorse. "You were right when you called us even," he explained gently. "After last night I realize how powerfully the subconscious can motivate emotions as well as actions. I never meant to hurt you, but I did."

She gritted her teeth and looked up at him with a calm she was far from feeling. "And I never meant to hurt you, but I did. So where," she asked, holding her breath in fear of his answer, "do we go from here?"

His eyes narrowed as he studied her face. "Do you want our marriage to continue?"

She nodded, the strength of her emotions beyond voiced expression. Afraid of the hesitation that followed her silent admission she reached for his hand and felt his fingers thread through her own as he returned to her side. With a last look into her dark, troubled eyes he bent forward and kissed her with a tenderness that broke apart her mute despair.

She whispered against his mouth, her voice thick with misery. "I don't want anything to change between us, Rob."

"Then we won't let it, Sharon!"

Although Sharon clung to Rob's promise in the weeks that followed there were drastic changes in their relationship that she found impossible to ignore. She couldn't fault Rob's behavior toward her, and yet she eventually realized that was a large part of the problem. He was considerate and always thoughtful of her wishes. Sharon knew anyone else would think her insane, but his unfailing kindness was driving her crazy.

They no longer disagreed on anything. Many times she tried to coax him into one of the teasing skirmishes they used to enjoy, but he didn't respond as he had in the past. Instead he agreed with her, and she was left feeling frustrated and resentful. It seemed their relationship had been locked inside an emotional freezer, and she could no longer depend on Rob for the warmth she needed.

Sharon's health didn't help their relationship. Her pregnancy was beset by difficulties she hadn't anticipated, and she was forced to leave the running of the restaurant to Claudia much earlier than she'd planned. Toward the end of her seventh month she felt sick more often than not, and her feet became so swollen it was difficult to distinguish her toes. Sometimes she wondered what would happen if she stuck a pin into her legs. She could see herself deflating like a hot air balloon, yet when she mentioned her theory to Rob he wasn't amused.

"You haven't developed toxemia yet, but there's always the possibility, Sharon. I want you to rest as much as you can during the day," he said, his voice so coolly professional she felt like decking him.

"Have you forgotten the party tonight?"

Rob frowned and nodded his head. "I had forgotten," he admitted with an exasperated grimace. "I'll call and send our apologies."

His automatic assumption that they should stay home made her angry. "I want to go to the party, Rob."

He reacted to the demand in her voice with marked impatience. "I know you're bored being alone all day with nothing to do, but a dinner and dance isn't a very sensible alternative, Sharon."

Rob sat beside her on the couch and put his arm around her shoulders. She didn't resist when he pulled her against his side, although he must have been aware of the tension in her body. "Why don't I go pick up some Chinese food and bring back a couple of tapes for the VCR?''

He was trying to pacify her as though she were a child, and Sharon felt her anger accelerate. With a mocking laugh she pulled away from him and glanced around the living room with obvious resentment. "What a brilliant way to get me out of this prison!"

"Sharon, I understand how you feel, but—"

"But what?" she interrupted shrilly. "But going out for a few hours is against doctor's orders?" Sharon clenched her fists together and glared at him. "For one thing, you can't possibly understand how I feel, staring at the same walls day after day," she continued distractedly. "For another, I was under the impression you were my husband, not my physician."

At the end of his patience, Rob's reply was succinct and to the point. "Am I to be condemned for using a little common sense?"

"Oh, what's the use?" she remarked tiredly. She leaned her head against the back of the couch and closed her eyes. "The way I look right now I'm better off at home where no one can see me anyway."

Rob uttered a curse and jumped up to stand in front of her. "Don't talk like an idiot," he exclaimed harshly. "If pregnant women repelled me I would have chosen to practice a different field of medicine. You're not unattractive, Sharon."

Sharon's mouth assumed a grim slant as she opened her eyes to look up at him. "Since we hardly ever make love anymore, I find it hard to believe you still find me physically appealing."

A whole gamut of emotions was reflected on Rob's face, the uppermost astonishment. "The way I remember it you were the one who indicated my advances were unwelcome."

"Do you expect me to enjoy making love to a man who ignores me until we climb into bed?"

"I spend as much time with you as I can," he said through gritted teeth.

"Don't do me any favors," she retorted. "I don't want you to feel obligated to do your husbandly duty. There should be more to lovemaking than just going through the motions."

Rob flushed and ran an impatient hand through his hair. "I still desire you, Sharon."

The stilted admission made her want to cry. "Is that why you make excuses to delay coming to bed until you're sure I'm asleep?"

"I've brought work home before and you never complained," he remarked defensively. "What is it you want from me, for God's sake?"

"I want us to be the way we were, can't you understand that?"

Suddenly Rob's shoulders slumped and he turned to stare outside at the darkness. "We can't go back to the way we were," he said softly. "I only wish we could."

"You . . . you've stopped loving me?"

He whirled to face her. "I didn't say that," he blurted.

She gripped the arm of the couch until her fingers ached. "Then what are you trying to say?"

"Why do you expect me to find an easy answer to a problem I didn't create? I want you, but when we make love something's missing, Sharon."

"The only thing missing is trust," she said softly. "Oh, Rob, why can't you believe in my love for you?"

"How can I, when every time I touch you I feel you cringe away from me?" he asked. "I don't want to have to seduce you into responding to me in bed."

Sharon lowered her eyes to the floor. They had caused each other so much pain that she wondered if she would ever again find her sandcastle man inside the stranger Rob had become.

Dear God, she thought, as he returned to his brooding stance by the window. When would they stop misunderstanding each other? Wasn't there some way to regain trust and put away resentment—some way to bridge the distance between them? With this thought in mind Sharon rose and approached him hesitantly. "The only reason I stiffened up on you was because I felt ugly, Rob. I'm sorry if I made you think I didn't want you to touch me."

He turned and his eyes were shadowed as he looked down at her. "Is that the truth, Sharon?"

She nodded, her eyes filling with tears. "Do you believe me?"

He studied her expression and said, "I think it's time we put the past behind us and learned to believe in each other, don't you?"

"It's what I want more than anything," she admitted softly. "I'm sorry if I made you think differently, Rob."

"I'm the one who's sorry," he said. "I guess I forgot to tell you how beautiful you look as you grow big with my child."

She laughed tremulously and gave him a relieved grin. "Big being the operative word?"

His eyes were drawn to the curve of her mouth, and Sharon caught her breath at the intense look on his face. She felt poised on a pinnacle, and she longed to find the closeness they'd once shared. With agonizing hesitancy she stepped forward, unaware of the silent appeal in her dark gaze.

When Rob drew her close she rested her cheek against his broad chest with a sigh of relief. She felt him draw a deep breath as he said gently, "The operative word is beautiful."

Sharon wanted to tell Rob she loved him. She wanted to tell him she only felt beautiful when he held her. The words were there in her mind, but she was afraid to speak them aloud. To actually voice her feelings could break apart this precious moment, and as she savored the sensation of his strong arms around her, she knew she wasn't brave enough to risk another rejection. So she remained silent while the warmth of his body eased a small portion of the chill encasing her heart.

Dr. Lawrence Mason looked down at the papers scattered on top of his desk and glanced over his glasses at Rob and Sharon. "The tests were positive, Rob. Sharon has developed toxemia, and I'd like her admitted to the hospital this afternoon."

Rob nodded, his expression grim. "I have her things in the trunk of the car, Larry."

"The baby's not due for another month," Sharon protested. She glanced away from Rob's tight-lipped face and gave her attention to her doctor. "Why must I be admitted this early?"

The note of fear in her voice didn't go unnoticed. Dr. Mason cleared his throat loudly before he gave her his most benevolent smile. "Since Rob's the one in danger of having his fingers crushed I'll let him explain."

Rob waited until Sharon looked at him before saying, "Toxemia's dangerous for both you and the baby if not kept under control, Sharon. You need to stay completely off your feet to conserve energy. Only in the hospital can your blood be monitored and the proper treatment be given to ensure your well-being."

"I'm not worried about myself," she said on the verge of tears. "What about our child, Rob?"

"The baby will be fine as long as you rest and take proper care of yourself, honey."

Sharon looked at Dr. Mason, who nodded and smiled his reassurance. Giving him a stilted grin in return she made a move to stand. Even with Rob's assistance the effort was exhausting, and her breathing was rapid and shallow as she leaned against her husband's side. "You're both right," she admitted, struggling for breath. "Staying in bed sounds heavenly."

A wheelchair was brought to her as soon as she left the office, and the relief she felt at not having to walk was enormous. The paperwork had already been dealt with by Rob and only needed her signature. Then she was taken upstairs and settled into a pleasant, if impersonal, room and was asleep as soon as her head touched the pillow.

Sharon wasn't allowed to rest for long. Being run through a battery of tests wasn't her favorite way to spend an afternoon, although she did enjoy the attention she received from the nurses who popped in periodically to tease her about Rob. He was obviously a great favorite, and when he arrived to visit her she couldn't let such a golden opportunity pass.

"Being the wife of a good-looking young doctor does have its advantages," she teased. "Not only do I hear all the latest gossip, but you don't have to stick to visiting hours."

"You're certainly feeling smug, woman." His eyes darkened as he reached for her hand. "If you want me with you just ring the desk. I've left instructions that I'm to be called no matter what the hour."

Sharon shifted onto her side to get a better view of her husband. "You need your rest as much as I do, Rob. I'm not going to send for you in the middle of the night if I get depressed."

"That's just what I want you to do, honey," he insisted, lifting her hand and placing a kiss against her palm. "I'll be bunking here for the duration, so I won't be far away."

"You'll do no such thing, Robert Barnes!"

"I will, too."

"You will—" Sharon caught her breath with a sob. "We're arguing," she whispered disbelievingly.

Rob shook his head, and the smile he gave her made words unnecessary. "I thought we called it making love, Princess."

Sharon tried to hear the whispers. A deep voice rose above the sound of a scream, but she couldn't make out what was said. She had retreated from the pain and though the darkness of unconsciousness was a blessed haven, she knew she would be lost if she didn't listen to the words being spoken.

"Can you hear me, Princess?"

Sharon's eyes were closed as she tried to recognize the voice penetrating the shadows. It didn't sound like Rob, she thought, and yet he was the only one who would call her Princess. She felt her lashes flutter against her cheeks as she struggled to open her eyes. Slowly her eyelids lifted, and the mists shrouding her mind were dispersed as she focused on her husband's face.

"The baby," she whispered. "They're going to save my life by taking our baby's, aren't they?"

"Everything's going to be all right."

Rob bent closer, and as he wiped the perspiration from her face with a cool cloth, Sharon saw fear in his eyes. "Don't lie to me, Rob."

"I'm not lying," he exclaimed harshly. "You and the baby are going to be fine. Larry is ordering the operating room prepared for a cesarean section."

At that moment another man appeared at Rob's side and Sharon recognized Lawrence Mason. "Do you know what's happening, Sharon?"

She twisted her head restlessly and reached for Rob's hand before trying to reply. "I'm losing the baby."

Larry's face came closer, and he stilled Sharon's movements with a gentle touch. "You haven't lost your baby, Sharon. You're too weak to continue labor and we have to take him surgically."

"Will he be all right?"

"Your infant's going to be fine."

Larry glanced toward Rob. "Will you assist?"

Sharon gripped Rob's hand, but she needn't have worried. "Yes," he said, "but I'll wait to prep. I want to stay with my wife until she's wheeled into surgery."

The doctor agreed and left them alone. It was then Sharon cried out against the agony of another pain, one that seemed to go on forever. She heard Rob's voice soothing her from an even greater distance than before and knew she had to speak to him while she was still able. With all of her available willpower she concentrated on the strength of his hand and pulled herself from the threat of unconsciousness.

"Rob, I love you."

She saw tears flood his eyes, and she stared up at him wonderingly. "Why are you crying?"

"Because you love me, and because I've been a blind, stupid fool with more pride than sense."

He sat beside her and lowered his head to her breast. "I love you so much, I'd die without you," he whispered.

"But if it comes to a choice," she gasped, "I want the baby to live."

"You can't ask that of me," he protested, lifting his head and closing his eyes to block out the pleading expression on her pain-wracked features. "I need you more than life itself, Princess. How can you expect me to . . . ?"

His voice broke, and Sharon reached out to caress his cheek. She brushed away the dampness clinging to her fingertips and was suddenly unafraid to confront the future. With a serene smile she cradled his face in her hands, confident of her ability to reassure the man she loved.

When his lashes lifted to reveal the clear, loving light in his eyes, she said, "I don't need to ask you to choose. As long as you're with me, everything will be fine."

Sharon's eyes closed, and she was comforted by Rob's fierce declaration. "I won't let anything happen to either of you, my sweet love!"

Rob kept his promise. Sharon was given an epidural anesthetic and when the numbing injection took effect she was able to smile at her husband with all the love she felt for him in her eyes. That love increased a thousandfold when she saw the awestruck expression on his face as their baby daughter was held up for their inspection. The baby's tiny fists flailed the air as she squalled with indignation at being thrust so suddenly into the world.

Although premature, Melissa Lynn Barnes weighed in at five pounds, six-and-a-half ounces, and even Larry admitted she had as healthy a pair of lungs as he'd ever heard. "Now maybe you'll quit worrying and get some rest," he said gruffly, "and the same goes for my esteemed colleague."

"I'm all right," Rob protested, his hand still gripping Sharon's. "I want to stay with my wife."

She tugged on his fingers until he bent over her. "Rob, you need to sleep," she whispered.

He kissed the smile from her mouth. "You're only worried because you love me."

It was then Sharon knew their love for each other had been tested by fire and had emerged strong and beautiful. They had learned to trust in their feelings, and there would no longer be a reason to struggle alone through the shifting sands of doubt and pride. She looked into his beautiful eyes and knew they shared one heart, one soul and dreams of castles in the sand.

As Rob feathered a kiss against her mouth, she murmured, "I adore you, my sandcastle man."

His laugh was joyful. "That's why you gave me exactly what I wanted, Mrs. Barnes."

Sharon's eyes widened. "But you wanted a boy!"

"I did not," he retorted, a wicked gleam vying with the adoration in his gaze.

"You did, too!"

 **Silhouette Desire**

COMING NEXT MONTH

EYE OF THE TIGER—Diana Palmer
Eleanor had once loved Keegan—handsome, wealthy and to the manor born. The differences between them were great, and time hadn't changed them. But the passion was still there too.

DECEPTIONS—Annette Broadrick
Although Lisa and Drew were separated, the movie stars agreed to make a film together. Would on-camera sparks rekindle passionate flames off-camera as well?

HOT PROPERTIES—Suzanne Forster
Sunny and Gray were rival talk-show hosts, brought together in a ratings ploy. Their on-air chemistry sent the numbers soaring—but not as high as Sunny's heart!

LAST YEAR'S HUNK—Marie Nicole
Travis wanted to be known for his acting, not his biceps.
C. J. Parker could help him, but business and pleasure don't always mix . . . and she had more than business in mind.

PENNIES IN THE FOUNTAIN—Robin Elliott
Why was Megan James involved with big-time crook Frankie Bodeen? Detective Steel Danner had to know. He'd fallen in love at first sight, and he was determined to prove her innocence.

CHALLENGE THE FATES—Jo Ann Algermissen
Her child might be alive! Had Autumn and Luke been victims of a cruel lie—and could they pick up the pieces and right the wrongs of the past?

AVAILABLE THIS MONTH:

READERS' COMMENTS ON SILHOUETTE DESIRES

"Thank you for Silhouette Desires. They are the best thing that has happened to the bookshelves in a long time."

—V.W.*, Knoxville, TN

"Silhouette Desires—wonderful, fantastic—the best romance around."

—H.T.*, Margate, N.J.

"As a writer as well as a reader of romantic fiction, I found DESIREs most refreshingly realistic—and definitely as magical as the love captured on their pages."

—C.M.*, Silver Lake, N.Y.

"I just wanted to let you know how very much I enjoy your Silhouette Desire books. I read other romances, and I must say your books rate up at the top of the list."

—C.N.*, Anaheim, CA

"Desires are number one. I especially enjoy the endings because they just don't leave you with a kiss or embrace; they finish the story. Thank you for giving me such reading pleasure."

—M.S.*, Sandford, FL

*names available on request